The Bears

Katie Welch

Copyright © 2012 by Katie Welch
Cover and illustration by Dylan Stinson
All rights reserved.

ISBN: 1-4793-0787-4
ISBN-13: 978-1-4793-0787-6
Library of Congress Control Number: 2012917334
CreateSpace Independent Publishing Platform
North Charleston, South Carolina

to Will Stinson
with love

Acknowledgements

First and foremost I would like to thank my daughters, Olivia and Heather Hughes, for their unwavering love and support. Special thanks also to Thomas A. Brown, teacher and friend. Tom, you nurtured and informed a love for nature and the outdoors in me thirty years ago. You are the original inspiration for this book; may the Great Bear bless you. Dylan Stinson, for your fabulous artwork, insight, and vision, thank you! Respect and many thanks to Scott, my editor at CreateSpace, thanks as well to my team at CreateSpace. Gratitude and thanks to the great teachers and friends who have put their faith in me. Your confidence in my abilities has sustained me through the years: Donna & Paul Bishop, Leslie & Todd Collier, Fred Flahiff, Norman Handy, J. Douglass Hume, Jeff & Heather Hilberry & the Hilberry clan, Sidney Katz, Elizabeth McCullough, Shelly

McKerchar, Sheldon Shore, Julie Threinen. Thank you also to my family, especially my brother Tim Welch and my sister Maureen Welch, who have always encouraged me to write.

Thank you to everyone working to protect nature and wilderness around the world and especially in northern British Columbia.

I have dedicated this book to Will Stinson, but his name needs to be here as well because without his love, help, faith, encouragement, and support, The Bears would still be in my head and not in your hands.

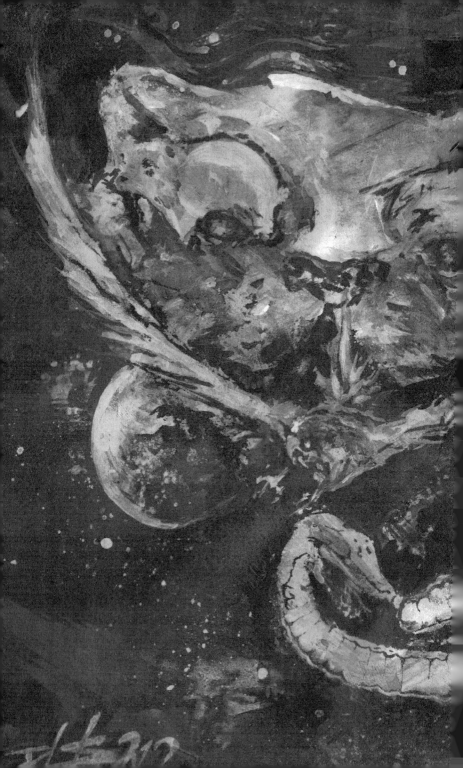

"Who trusted God was love indeed
And love Creation's final law
Tho' Nature, red in tooth and claw
With ravine, shriek'd against his creed"

—In Memoriam A.H.H., Canto 56
Alfred, Lord Tennyson

The Bears

The Great Bear Creates the World

In the beginning there was only the Great Bear. Everything was dark because when the Great Bear opened her eyes her head was tucked into her own belly, and she saw only the dark blackness of her own fur. The Great Bear then knew herself, and she knew she was alone. Keeping her head tucked into her black-furred belly, she licked and licked until her fur lay flat in one spot. The Great Bear then extended one long, sharp claw and drew it across this spot. Little beads of blood formed along this line, and these drops fell down and became the Black Bears of the earth.

With her eyes firmly shut, the Great Bear unfolded herself and stood over her Black Bears. She realized that she had to move her bowels and she did so, squatting on her rear haunches and releasing little pellets. These fell down and became the Brown Bears of the earth.

The Great Bear breathed in, and with the intake of her breath she created the wind. She exhaled and the moisture from her breath created the rain. Then the Great Bear at long last opened her eyes, and this created light—a great, blinding flash of pure white light. The Great Bear's eyes watered with this sudden exposure to light, and these tears fell down and they became the White Bears of the earth. Because they did not fall under the Great Bear's body they were not warm, and the place where the White Bears fell remained white and cold and frozen.

The Great Bear looked beneath herself at the Black, White, and Brown Bears and she was pleased with her creations. She saw wind ruffle their fur and she saw rain slake their thirst. She saw that the bears had no home, and in that moment she felt that she was about to give birth to a cub. The Great Bear then gave birth to the small bear, which she named Earth. If you look up in the night sky, you will see Ursa Major, the mother of us all, and Ursa Minor, our mother's cub, which is also our home.

The Great Bear gently took the Black Bears of the earth in her mouth and put them on her cub's back. Then she carefully took the Brown Bears of the earth in her mouth and put them on her cub's stomach. She took the White Bears of the earth, as well as their frozen environs, and put them on her cub's tail. The Great Bear saw that all of her bears moved comfortably on the surface of her cub. She then sent her cub to walk among the stars.

Tlingit

Hungry. I am ravenous. I think about my own teeth scraping at my insides, my bleeding insides, eating blood, so hungry I eat my own insides. Sharp yellow teeth itching for crunch and suck of seal bone. Edges of whiteness are seeping red. Where can Tlingit find seal—sweet, sweet seal meat? Think of the first claw ripping open soft fur. Think of jelly fat inside mouth and inside throat, moving fast past teeth sore from seal skull crushing.

Slowly moving and moving slowly over brown-grey-not-white. Where once was white of snow, now only brown of rock. Brown-grey-not-white holds nothing, strange hot sharp rock, strange lack of white. The edges of where whiteness should be seeping red. High sun hot why? Sun high and hot. I return, turn and re-turn, return to find big cold empty water with maybe fish, maybe seal. Seal swimming faster, slipping away, no hiding on cold hard ice and surprising seal.

Hungry I am, ravenous.

Moksgm'ol

The River Spirit has been generous this warm time. This long strong fish flailing in my jaws is for sport only. There must be thirty like it in my belly—belly full of fat pink flesh. I release this fish to the smooth round stones at my front claws. It arches, silver red scales flashing, slit eyes bulging in the air. I let it thrash three times, four times, five, scales now shredding onto rocks, rips and tears splitting its tail.

A sudden massive thrash and this new fish distances itself from me, flipping and flopping down and toward the water, red pink flashing, Fish Spirit attempting to join the clear, winking blue-grey Water Spirits again. Not permissible, for am I not Moksgm'ol?

Moksgm'ol of the forest, announcing my presence with creamy white fur flashes through green after green, bough upon bough, moss and rock, rain and branch, sun and wind! Moksgm'ol who eats—nay, feasts—at my leisure and my pleasure! Moksgm'ol, Keeper of Dreams, Keeper of Memory! Moksgm'ol who reigns, shining white crown, stalking unhindered throughout my Great Rainforest Kingdom!

Yukuai (Happy)

First I smelled the bamboo—so much fresh bamboo, crispy green sugar smells, so many—and through the grasses I pushed toward the smells-which-mean-deli-

cious. Now I remember another smell too, some strange, sick perfume.

Ling Ling was behind me, I felt her but the bamboo smelled so good. Later, I learned that Pyung, En Lai, and Chiu Chiu were also nearby, lured by the fresh food smells also and captured in the same way.

When the oh-so-sweet bamboo was close, the grasses were close also—too close I think now—a tunnel of bamboo and grasses made by the deathmen, leading into the hard black-barred-box. Later, when all of the green grasses browned and the bamboo died and fell away, I saw I was in a black-barred-box. The fresh bamboo we had not seen for a month had been placed inside these boxes to trick us.

Juicy flesh of bamboo squirting under my teeth—I ate three, four bites before the stink and sound of the death-men came. An ugly gong sound clanged and then the grasses and bamboo would not move. I pushed with limbs, bit with jaws, ripped with claws. The grasses had stiff, immovable parts that did not yield to bite or slash. These were the black bars of the box.

For some time I believed that Good Fortune was with me that day. She compelled my stomach and urged me to gorge on the bamboo. I saw nothing of the deathmen until I was properly snared beyond escape.

For some time I believed En Lai was not smiled on by Good Fortune that day. He turned before the black bars closed behind him and the deathmen smote him with long sticks. Perhaps this hurt. I don't remember hearing En Lai call out in pain. His moans came later when the grasses had died and I could see him lying on his side in a black box like mine.

Now I know better. Good Fortune smiled on En Lai. She opened her gold- stitched red robes, smiled her small, enigmatic smile, and released the deathmen with their sticks to slash at his belly. He died quickly; he never knew all the black-barred-boxes of the Great Wide World or the legions of white-faced deathmen outside of them looking in.

The Great Bear Creates People

It was summer and the Brown Bears of the earth were very, very warm. The year's cubs began to cry because they were so hot, and they begged their mothers to cool them down. The mothers taught their cubs to swim, as was the way when the sun shone so brightly and their fur was too warm. The mothers taught the cubs to lie on the earth in the shade of the green leafy trees. It was no use, though—nothing cooled off the cubs enough and so they cried and cried.

The Great Bear heard the incessant crying of the cubs of the Brown Bears of the earth. The Great Mother took pity on these cubs, reaching down and licking them with her great tongue to cool them off. But when the Great Bear licked the Brown Bear cubs, all of their fur came off and they were naked. The cubs were happy then, and they ran here and there, their pale skin growing pink and then red under the intense sun. Soon enough, they realized that they had painful sunburns and the cubs began to cry again in earnest.

The Brown Bear mothers heard their cubs crying, and they went to find them. When the bear mothers saw these pinkish red creatures, they did not recognize them as their own children. At this point, the cubs' crying had attracted other predators. Wolf was there, as well as Coyote. Cougar was lurking nearby. Overhead, Eagle was circling, anticipating a feast.

The Great Bear saw that all of the naked cubs would soon be eaten if she didn't intervene. She had to act quickly to save their lives. She pulled all of the cubs up onto their hind legs, took away their tails, and gave them the gift of intelligence so that they could escape from their enemies. With the blessing of intelligence came the curse of self-consciousness, and the cubs, realizing that they were naked, grew ashamed. They ran and hid themselves in the bushes.

That's right, run and hide, little naked ones, said the Great Bear. Be cunning and do not show yourselves. Walk lightly and quietly on the earth so that your enemies will not hear you. Use the abundance of the earth to feed yourselves, to stay warm in the winter, and to house yourselves and your young.

The constellation *Boötes*, wide at the shoulders and narrow at the feet, stands upright to represent People in the heavens.

Moksgm'ol

I, the mighty Moksgm'ol, move lazily toward the fish I do not want to eat. Its thrashes are still powerful, but my jaws will close around its silver sides and end its life. Then there is movement upriver—a rippling presence in the thick tall cedars. I turn my head from the fish, raise my head, and flare my nostrils. Who dares interrupt Moksgm'ol mid-feed?

I do not discover who dares. The pierce of Eagle's shriek blasts from over my head. I turn back in time to see Eagle's perfect arc, his vast wings spread as he swoops down from a tall treetop. His talons penetrate the fish—my fish, the fish of Moksgm'ol—at the nadir of his dive. He then soars to the zenith of a new green perch far above me.

I release my jaw and roar my complaint. But Eagle knows he has deceived me. He settles on a cedar snag within my sight and begins to eat my fish with impudence high above me. He tears at the pink flesh with his savage yellow beak and raises his white head to gulp the meat down his gullet.

I turn my creamy backside to Eagle and walk slowly away, my paws squishing in the carcasses of my salmon kills. Moksgm'ol has plenty and will catch plenty more. The river-banks are rank and red with the remains of my meals.

Gilbert

Before the disaster struck, he knew that it would be coming soon, but he was powerless to stop it. It was like trying to raise your fist during an ambush with your arms tied behind your back. All you can do is tense up and prepare for the blow.

He woke up four times that night. It was the worst night he had spent since the night he had heard that the project had passed and the pipeline would go through. The Black Snake of Death would soon undulate through the forest. Formal talks, negotiations, protests, news reports, and public outcry—all of this had been futile. Big money had—as the cynics had predicted—won. Poison would be pulled from the earth and sucked from the depths where it safely lay. This poison would then be processed to increase its toxicity. Land and forest would be rent asunder to allow the Black Snake of Death to wind its way to the Great Water. The viscous black blood of the Black Snake of Death would then be sent by boat to the people who hungered for it.

In the pale light of dawn, Gilbert slipped into the jeans that he seemed to have shed only minutes earlier. A favourite blue plaid flannel shirt hung over the chair by his bed. He put this on too, as well as some grey woollen socks that his sister Jean had knit for him. At fifty-two degrees of latitude, the month of September was less like autumn and more like early winter. The sting of northern winds was like a series of surprising and playful slaps, like cold hands against sun-warmed brown cheeks.

Gilbert shuffled across the wooden floors of his house. He filled the black kettle and slid it noisily onto the cast-iron top of the wood stove. Smoke sighed out of the front of the stove as he opened it, and the hinges squeaked. Orange embers were still dancing inside. He added a little more wood and a few more sticks of fuel—the bare minimum required for boiling water. He added the wood a little sadly and mumbled his gratitude to the Creator. He gave thanks for this fuel, this heat, and this source of life and living. Energy took many forms, Gilbert had learned, and clever people always imagined more forms of fuel. But demands for energy increased exponentially with the cold and hunger of a global population of ever-increasing billions.

There were dirty forms of energy and clean forms. The clean ones were simple and the Creator offered them freely. The sun offered warmth with orange hands, sending it down to be captured and enjoyed without stipulation. Opening their soft green arms, the great cedars of the forest flourished and thrived by capturing this fuel. The great lips of the Creator blew steady winds that wise Eagle used to his advantage, capturing the fuel of movement under his brown and white wings. Ocean tides surged in and out. There was so much kinetic energy and fuel that was freely given.

This wood that was burning in his stove with little flames licking at its sides was a hundred-year-old tree. The tree had been struck down for the fuel inside of her. This grand old lady of the forest shed her grey, sooty robes of ash to remind those benefitting from her time-accrued energy—the efforts of all of her years—that she was a dirtier fuel, dirtier than the sun's warm hands or the wind's fresh breath. When she stored energy in trees the Creator had not given her fuel away freely, it came at an environmental price. But the Creator had also not relinquished her fuel as reluctantly as she had when she buried oil, the black blood of the Black Snake of Death.

After a breakfast of fish and buttered toast, Gilbert went on a walk to the riverbank. The sunlight was growing brighter. He shut his front door cautiously, unwilling to mar the sparkling gem of morning with a boorish slam. He stretched out on the front porch, his long muscular brown limbs extending almost to the ceiling. His chestnut-brown, straight hair fell evenly down to his waist. He often wore it in a single braid, but today he was eager to walk, so he tied it impatiently into a loose ponytail.

With two big strides, Gilbert descended the four wooden steps and set off on his accustomed river-bound trail through the forest. He walked at a quicker-than-usual, anxious pace, edgy with sleeplessness and worried about how much worse the forest would be since the pipeline had been constructed.

Over a long enough timespan, there was a one-hundred-percent chance of an accidental rupture or a spill occurring. The fragile and unique ecology of the coastal temperate rainforest would be irreparably damaged for the foreseeable future.

Birds would be rendered flightless, slick black chemical sludge encasing their feathers and destroying the miracle of flight. Fish would be choked with foreign poison. Some of them would die immediately, while others would carry smaller—though still deadly—quantities of that hated black goo within them for the spirit bear to consume in increments. Although he was at the top of the food chain, Moksgm'ol, the spirit bear, would die the most insidious death. Some chemical-induced cancer would eat away at his unique biology from the inside.

Gilbert and the Haisla people had made arguments, done research, and referenced ancient knowledge in order to stop the snake from coming. This hadn't been enough to stop the pipeline from being built, but their cumulative intelligence still existed. It danced incessantly inside of Gilbert's head. No wonder he couldn't sleep. Gilbert wasn't alone in his terror-induced insomnia. Gary and Sandra, Gilbert's best friends, both confessed to waking in cold sweats from dreams of oozing pools of black sludge.

This golden fall morning shouldn't be so poignant, Gilbert thought bitterly. The crisp clean smell of giant red cedars, the smell of rain evaporating from billions of Sitka spruce needles, the undertones of moss, the worms at work in rotting vegetation, the salty ocean—these smells became secondary to the pungency of decaying fish as Gilbert approached the Kitimat River. The salmon had returned to spawn in record numbers that year, which was ironic considering that the industrial dockyard had recently been completed. The fish were here to spawn. They were here to create life and then die. The ships came to carry away a slow but almost certain death for ocean life, a cargo of toxic, unrefined oil.

The shady darkness of the surrounding trees receded as the narrow walking trail opened up along the riverbank. Gilbert felt a tingling sensation—a presence—so he hung back among the trees to observe. As he waited, the clear water gurgled and sloshed over the smooth stones, singing a unique song. The insects buzzed and chirped, and the birds rustled and called, adding their instrumentation to the chorus.

He saw a flash of creamy fur. Downstream, maybe forty meters away, was Moksgm'ol, the spirit bear. He hadn't appeared this close to Kitimat since before the construction had begun. Gilbert held his breath. The bear was a good-sized one. Gilbert guessed that it was probably male and probably close to three hundred pounds, which was the upper end of how much these unique animals weighed. Moksgm'ol was slapping at an injured salmon; the fish was writhing and flopping under his great muddy paws. Dozens of other salmon were scattered along the shore in various stages of death and decay.

Gilbert felt almost giddy with relief. He had often experienced sleeplessness when Moksgm'ol was nearby. His terrible fears of impending disaster and doom were perhaps just that—fears and nothing more. One had to hope for the best and avoid living in a perpetual state of paranoia. One could not simply expect the worst and wait in helpless terror for an environmental disaster to come.

Having caught sight of this spirit bear, Gilbert felt as if it had dropped a smooth, round river stone into the pond of his soul. His body remained motionless, but his spirit expanded. Ripples of happiness and enthusiasm passed outward from his self in waves that moved in every direction. The ripples moved three dimensionally—not just toward the points on the compass but also up into the air. They went up toward the blue, white, and grey sky and down into the earth beneath him.

As the worm beneath Gilbert's feet felt Gilbert's soul expand, it expanded each of its segments, pushing little clods of dirt and tiny stones into new air pockets. As the beetle felt Gilbert's soul expand, she scuttled up a green twig and waved her antennae around so that she could better receive vibrations. The Sitka spruce, the red cedar, the western hemlock, and the Douglas fir felt Gilbert's soul expand too. These grand ladies whispered their pleasure in the smooth susurration of needles brushing against each other.

Eagle felt the undulation of Gilbert's joy; he turned his head sharply in the Gilbert's direction. Eagle's lizard-like eyes darted sharply back toward the river. O Moksgm'ol, you greedy-guts, thought the eagle. I'll teach you not to play with your food. The eagle shrugged his powerful shoulders, made himself into an arrow, and dove from his perch, shrieking with delight and extending his crooked claws out to snag the still-flailing fish.

Tlingit

Big, cold, empty water. Water is wanting. Water wants its winter clothes of icy blue and white. Water is naked. Swim in water. Move slowly again slowly again slowly—rhythm of swimming paws pressing patterns into big cold empty water. When water is naked, swimming is long. Magic seals melted icy blue water clothes, disappeared in big cold empty water. The water has no edges and the space has no limits—no seals, no fish. Hungry I am.

Water edges there must be. Inside ribs scraping empty bloody guts. Tasting blood—blood from ravenous stomach tasting. Always seeing white at edge of water meeting sky. Move through water—emptier, colder. White edges stay far away always—never move close. White water clothes came closer with swimming some time ago. Now the sun comes lower and more, it pushes winter away.

Think about K'ytuk. Don't think about K'ytuk. Please, please forget little K'ytuk—the feel of K'ytuk inside me, below hungry belly, moving inside me below my hungry belly. Belly pains crunched my insides all day and then tiny, bloody K'ytuk outside my body. Lick blood from K'ytuk—lick and taste my body blood from new fur of my baby.

No think K'ytuk—heart hurting to think baby K'ytuk lost into warm waters not swimming, not breathing. Think any-thing, something, anything, to not remember how there was no end to the water and how K'ytuk could not...think not...think *of the old stories. Think something other—not pain, not water, not nothing-where-there-used-to-be-ice.*

Churchill Northern Studies Centre, Churchill, Manitoba

None of it had helped: the numbers, the statistics, the ratios, the research, the documentation, the photographs, the videos, and the reports. None of it was helping, and her sense of the futility of it all was growing, along with her anger.

Anne McCraig sat in the CNSC library shuffling her index cards and drinking herbal tea, afflicted with the torpor that had increasingly plagued her since Tlingit had returned without her cub. Ian Findlay and Jane Minoto—Doctor Jane Minoto, Anne mentally corrected herself—were capable of academically appraising the situation with detachment. Anne mentally capitalized it: the Situation. She was thinking about the Global Warming Situation, in which the animals that she had devoted her life to studying were starving and dying.

Anne closed her eyes and thought once again about Tlingit moaning as she stood on the shores of Hudson Bay, bereft at having lost her cub.

"Has it occurred to you," Anne had coughed to Jane through the tears and snot of grief, "that all we are doing is documenting their demise?"

"We are making a significant contribution to the scientific community regardless," Jane had answered, blinking rapidly as her face remained impassive.

"Contributions as what?" Anne had wailed. "Historians?"

"Drama won't help," Jane had intoned. "In any case, you don't know what happened to Tlingit's cub. You're drawing conclusions without any evidence to support them."

"Evidence? What more evidence do you need? There's thirty-five percent less ice this year than there was last year. They were starving when they left, and the cub was too weak to walk on its own. Tlingit was desperate."

"Once again, Anne, you anthropomorphize and project," Jane had answered, her voice sounding smarmy and reasonable to Anne. "This planet has been through huge temperature fluctuations in its long history. Your myopia is interfering with your objectivity."

I'd rather be shortsighted and have a heart than be a dispassionate little smudge like you, Anne thought, her mind snapping back to the present. She immediately felt guilty about the racist overtones of her thoughts. Dr. Jane Minoto was a slight, tidy woman of Japanese heritage. Anne also realized, slumping even lower in her seat, that she was jealous of the senior scientist's small, muscular body. Anne's curves were always threatening to become rolls of—let's face it—fat.

When she had applied to do her post-graduate research at the Centre in Churchill, Anne had fondly imagined herself striding over the subarctic, achieving a fitness level unprecedented in her thirty-five years of life. She had transformed from the pretty, chubby blonde girl who loved animals into the pretty-but-round teenager who was widely admired for her brains but chosen last for every team sport in gym. The teenager transformed into a young woman, a hopeless undergraduate endomorph who alleviated the stress of final exams with litres of cookie dough ice cream and greasy grilled-cheese sandwiches liberally dipped in ketchup. When I get out in the field, Anne thought repeatedly, all this will change. Outside doing actual research, moving my body. The world would see the muscular, intrepid Anne McCraig who had been pupating, waiting for her moment to arrive. Prior to her departure for Manitoba, Anne had even purchased—she blushed to think of it now—an outfit that was a size smaller than what she usually wore. She couldn't believe her own hubris.

Wapusk National Park wasn't the weight loss program that Anne had hoped it would be. She had been toiling in this remote shoreline community for over a year now, and she was in worse shape than when she had arrived. Collecting data in the field was such a small part of the work that she did. The majority of her work involved sitting in front of a computer with a tray of date squares and a pot of sweet tea at her dimpled elbow. In any event, she and her only potential—in her opinion—romantic interest at the Centre, Ian Findlay, had decided mutually and firmly to be nothing more than friends.

Ian Findlay was recognized for his good-natured approach toward work and life. Tall and gangling, the scientist exuded an air of benevolence and competence. Thirty-three years old and unmarried, he had devoted himself utterly to the study of botany and geology. Each of his romantic entanglements resembled each other: an initial courtship of laughter and the discovery of common interests, an intermediate time of increasing awkwardness as the compass needle of Ian's attention swung back to the magnetic zero of his scientific interests and curiosity, followed by an endgame of unreturned phone calls, bored sighs over desperate dinners, and lackadaisical lovemaking. Anne knew about Ian's history because of one late night at the research centre over a few glasses of wine. Jane had retired early that night, as she did every night. Ian and Anne, who both considered themselves terminally single, had compared awkward date stories. The hilarity and boisterousness had increased until Jane roused herself and asked them to be quiet and go to bed. The revellers had done so, eyes twinkling and lips twitching with suppressed mirth. A new friendship had formed.

Then came the heartbreak of Tlingit. Tlingit had emerged thin but victorious from her den early the previous spring. Polar bears often had two cubs in a given litter, but Tlingit had emerged with a single cub. He—a male, the biologists quickly determined—was the youngest, smallest polar bear cub that Anne had ever seen and the first she had seen outside of captivity. He was a pure white puffball with round imploring eyes. For Anne, he represented love, surrogate motherhood, and professional curiosity all somehow bundled up together with her own hopes, fears, and dreams.

"Don't make an emotional investment," Jane had admonished her.

Anne had related Jane's passionless imperative to Ian in the hope that her favourite colleague would concur that Jane was a nasty, cold fish.

"You do need to keep your professional distance," Ian had counselled.

Damn them both, Anne had thought. She proceeded to order photographic enlargements of Tlingit's precious offspring and pin them up in the common room. She named the cub K'ytuk and fretted about his welfare. Her logical, scientific mind kept its opinions quiet about what an increasingly inhospitable environment the north was becoming for polar bears.

It had happened early one day in June. Anne woke early, surprised by the sound of the howling wind. She lay in bed watching the erratic gusts of an unseasonable blizzard tossing snow back and forth outside of her window. Anne just knew that Tlingit was out there, hungry and desperate to feed K'ytuk. Mid-morning, Anne and Ian ventured out to the Hudson Bay shoreline. The wind and snow were so severe that they both wore ski goggles to protect their eyes. It was a bad day for fieldwork; Ian had consented to accompany Anne out of sympathy and solidarity.

Squinting through the snow, they could see that Hudson Bay was wild. The large steel-grey waves were tossing and heaving. Adult bears could easily drown out there; cubs would stand a much smaller chance. I hope they are on land right now, Anne had thought.

Later that afternoon, the snow and wind had stopped as suddenly as they had come. The dark clouds separated, revealing patches of pale blue-white sky. Once again, Anne implored Ian to walk with her out toward Tlingit's den in hopes of catching sight of her favourite bear and the small cub.

Ian had spotted her first. She was standing right at the shoreline, swaying, sniffing, and searching, her muzzle pointed out over the water. She was alone. Anne made a small choking sound, grasping Ian's forearm and squeezing him in distress. Then Tlingit had begun to vocalize. A long, moaning sound had emanated from her great, black-rimmed mouth. She tilted her head back and released a series of moans.

Ian had pushed Anne's hand away, scrambling to pull his video camera from his shoulder pouch to begin recording. Tlingit continued to alternately sniff out over Hudson Bay and toss her head back and moan. It was a heart-wrenching sound—a grieving, uncannily human sound. After recording for seven minutes, it became evident to Ian that the bear would continue this remarkable behaviour in very much the same manner. He decided that he had documented enough digital evidence. Anne was weeping silently, her open mouth mutely mirroring the mourning bear.

"It's a unique recording," Jane admitted, sitting inside at the Centre, watching the little image on Ian's camera, and listening to the strange sounds emanating from the mother bear. "Polar bears aren't vocalizers. Except for when they are growling in a play fight, chuffing in anger, or mating, they don't vocalize. I've never heard—or heard of—anything like this before. You don't know that it is grief, though."

"What do your instincts tell you, Doctor Minoto?" snapped Anne, teary-eyed.

Four months had elapsed since Ian had made the recording. Since then, Anne had watched and listened to the seven-minute clip hundreds of times. She had slowed it down, sped it up, and compared it with every other recorded polar bear vocalization that she could find. She would sit at her computer, watching, listening, grieving, and eating. She was consuming calories while Tlingit was unable to. She was growing wider while the bear was growing narrower.

The Great Bear Creates Pandas

t one time, all of the bears lived in peace on their part of Small Bear—the earth—not knowing of each other's existence. The White Bears of the earth lived far out in the cold of Small Bear's tail, the Brown Bears of the earth lived on Small Bear's warm tummy, and the Black Bears of the earth stayed on Small Bear's back.

Then came an exceptionally cold year, and the White Bears strayed farther down Small Bear's back than they ever had before in search of food. They wandered so far that they eventually strayed into the territory of the Black Bears. The Black Bears did not see the White Bears at first, as the Black Bears were hibernating and staying close to their dens. But Snake stirred early that year, and one morning, while warming his blood in the sun, Snake saw a White Bear for the first time.

Snake had grown bored after the long winter, so he decided to make some trouble. He slithered to the Black Bears' den and hissed that he had seen a bear bigger and much more beautiful than the black bear. He hissed that he had seen a pure white bear. The Black Bears were incredulous at first, but their natural curiosity overtook them, and eventually they followed Snake to the rocky place where the White Bears were harvesting berries from the shrubs that grew there.

The Black Bears growled and roared in anger at seeing their food supply being diminished by these intruders. Then the White Bears, whose stomachs were shrunken with hunger, growled and roared back. The Black Bears and the White Bears began fighting each other. Soon the rocky place was a blur of black fur and white fur as the bears grievously injured each other.

The Great Bear heard the commotion of the battle below. She bent her head down to the place on her cub where the battle was taking place, and she separated the White and Black Bears with her tongue, but one of each kind got caught between her teeth. The Great Bear then chewed and spat them out. When she looked down, she saw that she had made a new kind of bear that was both black and white, and that was the bear that we call Panda Bear. The Great Bear sent them to live on Small Bear's chest.

If you look up in the night sky, you can see Snake, the constellation also known as Draco, and Panda, which is also called Cepheus.

Yukuai

The bamboo fields of my homeland seem a dream to me now. Perhaps I am dreaming them. I imagine them as a kind of Heaven—a green, waving land of plenty, a fresh water place of food everywhere and always, as far as one can roam. The roaming itself must also be a part of paradise, lumbering wherever one wishes without impediment. Are these dreams or memories? If I could, I would ask Pyung or Ling Ling because they were part of the dream. It seems to me that they were there in the endless fields of bamboo. Pyung or Ling Ling, if they live, must be living some life similar to this one I am living now—this infinitesimal, limited life.

On cold black starry nights, I remember warm bodies like mine around me—an expanse of black and white fur. During cold nights here in this prison, I am surrounded only by cold air, sometimes damp with rain or frigid with frost and snow. I shiver. I wish more bodies like my own were somewhere close by.

Some nights the cold is so biting that it is almost intolerable. On nights like these I remember Die Nacht der Feuers, the Firenight. I remember the screams of a hundred animals, the inescapable heat, the machines of the deathmen roaring mechanically overhead. I remember the very foam of fear evaporating from my bared teeth and lips—the flames shooting upward everywhere, the clouds of smoke burning my throat and eyes. I remember the Firenight, and although there is a hard kernel of coldness inside of me, the mere memory of burning that night warms my skin and fur and I sleep.

Lothar Fuhrenmann – Cologne, Germany, February 1939

"You instructed me to purchase a lucrative attraction. The bear is healthy, and there are no other bears like it in Germany at present. I secured the damn panda at your behest. Do with the creature what you wish, but I will have my compensation," Lothar snapped, transferring the heavy black telephone to his left shoulder.

Greta Fuhrenmann entered Lothar's office just then, balancing a tea tray on the broad shelf of her breasts. Her face was inexpressive as she approached Lothar's desk and deposited the tray with a clatter in front of her husband's polished black boots, which were on top of the brown leather desk blotter.

"Quiet, fool," Lothar hissed at his wife. Then he yelled into the telephone, "Nein! Not you, Herr Gunn! My oaf of a wife! She constantly interrupts me." Lothar swung his long legs off the surface of his desk, narrowly missing the lunch, a grey boiled egg and a slice of blackened toast, that his wife had just delivered to him. He squinted and scowled at Greta, who stood round-shouldered and oblivious before his massive desk.

"I completed my part of the bargain. Do you have any idea how difficult negotiating with an Englishman is right now? It's a diplomatic nightmare. And Willoughby-Jones— the fool—wanted to charge more because two of the things died in transit. That's not my problem!" Lothar's angular face was white and pinched, his thin moustache pointing sharply downward above an angry frown.

Greta watched her husband as he listened to Herr Gunn. Lothar was frozen in anger, the telephone pressed to his head. The Fuhrenmanns remained in a tableau of motionless hostility for some minutes.

Lothar broke the stillness with a sudden harsh bark. "That is precisely what you will do. I'll give you two days to secure a minimum of half a dozen bookings for the bear. No more excuses. The war will proceed. Life will proceed. I will continue to owe my creditors. The panda eats its weight in bamboo and fruit every three days. Do you have any idea how expensive that is? Call me when you have the bookings." Lothar hung up sharply. He turned his white, beak-like nose toward his wife, nostrils quivering.

"What is it, Frau Fuhrenmann? You disturb me greatly."

"It is Happy, Herr Fuhrenmann," replied Greta. "He has vomited up what we fed him this morning."

"Clean it up, then, Frau," said Lothar between clenched teeth.

"Yes, Herr Fuhrenmann. I have cleaned it. However, the bear is acting unwell."

"Acting unwell," echoed Lothar. "How unspecific. Please explain."

"He is groaning and shaking his head, and he isn't moving much," Greta Fuhrenmann reported. She stood with her familiar attitude of heavy resignation before her husband's desk. Her dress, Lothar recalled, had been white and dotted with pale pink flowers at some time in the past. It was now a mottled grey. What had he done to anger God? His wife was a dowdy numbskull, his children were incorrigible, and his career was a joke. Each day he rose, washed, trimmed, combed, dressed, waxed, and polished. He said his prayers to ask forgiveness for whatever unfathomable sin he had committed. A great sin it was, thought Lothar, to bring upon me these burdens.

When Lothar swung his boots off the desk, they missed Greta's broad, pale face by only inches. She raised her eyebrows slightly and flinched. Lothar snapped his thin, severe blade of a hand into the air, threatening to strike her. On this occasion, Greta was lucky. Lothar was content with offering only a threat. He strode out of the office with his boots drumming out the rhythm of his anger.

Lothar marched out of his house and followed a gravel path to a padlocked gate on a two-meter-high chain-link fence. Barbed wire curled and bristled at the top of the fence. The proximity of this back entrance to the Kolner Zoo had appealed to Lothar Fuhrenmann when he had bought his house. Now, however, he wished he lived as far away as possible from the damn place; then he wouldn't be tempted to take on so many of the menial tasks and duties associated with the great dumb beasts. How cruel fate had been to lead him into this sorry excuse of a livelihood, displaying a menagerie to a soft-hearted, mush-brained populace. It was a mediocre profit margin at best. Lothar couldn't imagine why he should allow his income to dwindle by employing an incompetent fool to shove food through the bars each day. Did he not have Greta and the half-retarded issue of her womb at his disposal?

Gravel crunched under his boots as Lothar strode toward Happy's enclosure. The animal lay on its side, its white fur streaked with brown mud. Was it dead? After surviving a rough capture and transport, had the black-and-white beast chosen to give up now? No, the thing's sides were heaving. Lothar circled the bars until he was able to look into Happy's unfocused, bloodshot eyes.

"Ungrateful shit," hissed Lothar. The vomiting was likely due to the excessive fruit-to-bamboo ratio that Lothar himself had been insistent about. Of course, he would admit this to no one. The other large animals tolerated having inexpensive foodstuff replace their native diets, but that wasn't the case with this problematic cartoon of a creature.

The zoo wouldn't open for another hour. Lothar scanned over his shoulders. Satisfied that no human could see or hear him, he began to kick viciously at the bars of Happy's cage, interspersing his kicks with nasty utterances:

"Stupid, fucking, ungrateful shit!"

Happy the Panda did not move or turn his great head to consider what new source of unpleasantness was going on.

Yukuai

They used crunchy green bamboo to lure me from one black-barred box to the next. I learned that a move was imminent when they didn't feed me and I became weak with hunger. At these times, the spitting man would come and stand outside my box and make harsh, rattling sounds. There would be other men with him, sometimes yelling angrily and other times speaking in hushed tones.

Usually they move me in the darkness of night in a rolling machine baited with sweet bamboo. In my desperate, famished state, I would go wherever they wanted me to go: into the rolling man machine or anywhere else they placed familiar food from my homeland.

Before dawn, the metal doors of my moving prison would open and disgorge me into a new black-barred box, free of my own droppings and urine. The sun would rise and I would explore every corner of the foreign enclosure, searching for a weakness or a flaw—any kind of way out. Then the humans would arrive—whole crowds pushing, pointing, shouting, crying, spitting, and calling out.

In my dreams, I would return to clear streams of laughing water, fine mists of rain delicately irrigating green grasses and trees, and moisture from the sky revealing the nature of rocks and earth. With time, the dreams grew faint and infrequent.

I have been in this, what seems to be my final penitentiary, for a long time now without any movement or change. I somehow managed to leave the spitting man behind. For this small mercy, at least, I can be grateful.

Gilbert

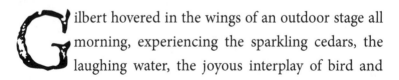 ilbert hovered in the wings of an outdoor stage all morning, experiencing the sparkling cedars, the laughing water, the joyous interplay of bird and

beast, the shore, and riverbank. He returned home some time after noon, walking slowly and quietly through the forest. After a brief lunch of cold water, bread, and fruit in his cabin, he went outside to split wood in the intense fall sunshine.

Gilbert loved the efficient ballet of the woodpile. He loved the upward heft of the axe or maul and the smooth wooden handle sliding almost freely between his calloused palms as it moved upward in a graceful parabola. He loved the decisive moment of gravity and intention at the apex of the swing. He loved the loud and gratifying whack of the metal wedge into the round of wooden rings. He loved the predictable direction of the hewn pieces of wood sent flying off in opposite directions. He loved the intermittent pauses when he stacked quantities of perfectly hewn wood into rows and pyramids of fuel.

Throwing his shirt carelessly aside, Gilbert's mind was quiet in its rhythmic labour. Such moments of idyllic perfection often pass unconsidered, but that was not the case this morning. Gilbert noted the gift of this day, and he captured it like a winged insect in amber. Within three days, he would recall its loveliness with sadness and regret. He swung his axe in the autumn of his own existence on the Great Mother. His grown children, Max and Charlotte, were also his friends. They lived nearby: Charlotte lived with her husband and child, and Max lived on his own. Their mother, Gilbert's wife Clara, had succumbed to cancer six years ago. These days, when Gilbert thought of Clara, he felt blessed about recalling the good times and not the illness. Charlotte was pregnant with his second grandchild. Jack, the first baby, was as boisterous and demanding of a grandson as anyone could wish for. Max worked at a tire shop in Kitimat.

The oil pipeline project had come along two years after Clara had died. Gilbert carried a good deal of anger and grief with him, which he turned toward the government, the oil company, and the people who approved of the pipeline. There were meetings to plan for and attend, protests to organize, and facts, statistics, and research to consider and compile. Ultimately, it had all been for naught. Then there was the gross affront and indignity of the actual construction of the pipeline. Some days, if the wind was coming from the northeast, Gilbert heard the grind and crunch of machinery and the crash of falling timber. He smelled diesel and dirt all day. The events were close enough in time that he couldn't help but compare them. Clara's death had been easier to handle.

None of these difficult thoughts crowded Gilbert's head that glorious autumn afternoon. His tawny skin shone with sweat. His taut muscles were engaged and defined. It was thusly that Gary and Sandra found him when they pulled up in front of the cabin in their small white pickup truck. The truck's faulty exhaust had already announced their visit to Gilbert, but he was loath to interrupt his meditative work. He continued swinging and whacking without acknowledging his friends' arrival.

"Maybe put your shirt on before my wife leaves me," intoned Gary from the open passenger window. Gilbert let the axe fall by his side, and he looked up grinning. Sandra was, in fact, openly appreciating Gilbert's sweaty shirtless torso.

"Water," said Gilbert. He hid his embarrassment by going into the cabin to get a T-shirt. When he came back two minutes later with three tall glasses of water, Gary and Sandra were sitting on the tailgate of their truck smoking. Gilbert distributed the water wordlessly. All three of them sat for some minutes without speaking, listening to the buzz of a chainsaw half a kilometer away and the sawing of crickets in the roadside grass.

"Cold winter coming," said Gary.

"Maybe." Gilbert cocked his head to one side and smiled at his friend.

"You're getting your wood in already. There must be a cold winter coming," Gary explained.

"Maybe," Gilbert said. "Maybe it's just a good day to split wood. What do you see from the sky these days?" Gary was a bush pilot. He often brought news about land being cleared, houses being built, or herds of deer passing through—inside information from the vantage of birds.

Gary shrugged. "Not much these days. There are more tankers anchored offshore than I've ever seen. Makes me damn nervous."

It made Gilbert nervous to think of the huge oil tankers navigating the winding archipelago in his backyard. "I'm done worrying," Gilbert lied.

"When is Charlotte's baby due?" asked Sandra.

"Soon," Gilbert answered. "Harvest moon."

"Any names?" Sandra arched an inquisitive eyebrow.

"River, for a boy. Ocean, for a girl." Gilbert grinned. "I suggested Eddy and Swell for middle names. Charlotte didn't think it was very funny."

"It's funny," Sandra laughed.

"If you want to fly with me before the snow comes, then you should come soon," Gary offered.

"Thanks," said Gilbert. "Maybe I will."

Gary and Sandra said goodbye and then climbed into their truck and started it. A cough of blue exhaust puffed into the street. Gilbert, disgusted, made a face and shooed them away with the back of his hand.

In the rear-view mirror, Sandra watched Gilbert pick up his axe and return to his woodpile. "He's lonely," she said. Gary nodded.

Birds and Bees

The smell in the air felled the bees. It fouled the bees. It confused, sickened, and grounded the bees. The birds flew away in fear.

The blade of the bulldozer had dislodged a rock that was nudged against another rock that had pounded into the pipeline without puncturing it. The pipeline was compromised, a dent pushed into the cylinder. Nothing happened immediately. To the construction crew working on the hotel and the housing complex above, nothing was visibly amiss.

Underground, however, the pressure was building. This surge of pressure found the path of least resistance and then—*pow, kablam*—there was a geyser. The pressure easily bored a hole through the meter of loosely packed earth above it. With a loud whoosh, a veritable gush of black gold spurted into the air.

It happened in the little forest between the Kitimat town centre and the Kitimat River. When a pipeline ruptures in the forest, does anybody hear it? Nobody heard it this time. Nighttime had descended and nearby businesses had closed for the day; the builders on the construction site had long since hung up their hard hats and headed home. The oil worked at the injury of the pipe, wearing away at the little compromised spot until it broke free.

Gilbert

The smell reached him in his dreams. He was dreaming about the days when the kids were small. In the dream it was summertime. He was pushing Max on a tire swing. Charlotte was suspended from a knotted rope on the far side of the massive tree that the tire dangled from. As Max kicked his dirty bare feet toward the clouds, his mouth was open and he was demanding, "Higher, daddy. Higher!" Charlotte's curtain of black-brown hair whooshed around her serene face. She was wearing that soft green dress that she had worn every day, it seemed, for a year or two. He could hear the sounds of other children laughing and screeching. A dog was barking incessantly. The noise of an internal combustion engine far away made a faint mechanical roar.

Max grew more insistent in the dream and then he became frustrated.

"Higher, Daddy. Higher. Higher!"

Gilbert was looking around and pushing the tire absent-mindedly. He was looking to see where that roaring engine sound was coming from. There must be a vehicle somewhere, but he couldn't see it. Suddenly, the smell of raw, dirty fuel grew pungent in the playground. Gilbert went from curious to perplexed. The engine sound seemed to be coming from everywhere and nowhere at the same time. "Higher, daddy. Higher!" screamed Max with an edge of hysteria in his voice. Gilbert turned around.

Oily, black tears were streaming down Max's face, coursing from his black-brown eyes. Two black lines of tears were beginning to stain the collar of the boy's yellow T-shirt. Gilbert looked at his daughter. She had stopped swinging, and she was merely hanging motionlessly with black rivulets flowing down her face as well and ruining her favourite green dress.

The overpowering smell of the fuel was choking him. Gilbert woke up gasping. He sat up and threw the covers off of his body. He was no longer dreaming. The smell of oil was permeating his whole house and outside there were more vehicles and voices than there should have been.

"Oh no. Oh no." Gilbert grabbed his jeans, ripped a shirt from his closet, pushed his feet into runners, and stumbled outside, his hair wild from tossing and turning. His eyes were giant, black, foreboding orbs. "No, no, no."

Gary was sitting in his truck in front of Gilbert's house. The truck engine was idling. For one crazy moment, Gilbert felt a sick, angry relief as he decided that maybe Gary's truck exhaust had caused the powerful stench. But across the street, his neighbours were standing in their front yards, talking, looking toward town, and glancing back at Gilbert's cabin. Everyone knew how hard Gilbert had fought the pipeline. Then came the sound of a siren. Three trucks passed in succession. It was high traffic for this street.

Gary's face was a flat, impassive mask. Gilbert's stomach clenched as he gasped, his lungs tight and unresponsive. It had happened already. This soon after the construction of the pipeline, the disaster that they had tried to avert had come. With his legs pushing him forward, Gilbert silently got into the truck beside his friend.

At less than five minutes, the drive was short. They headed slightly west of downtown on Haisla Boulevard toward the bridge that spanned the Kitimat River. There they saw a semicircle of haphazardly parked emergency vehicles, fire trucks, and police cars blocking access to a housing development that was under construction beside a little strip mall. Spindly wooden frames—some of them partially covered in particleboard—were spread out on an expanse of brown mud. On the street beside the emergency vehicles, people stood in knots. Some of them were frowning and some were weeping; most of them were holding shirts or scraps of fabric over their mouths and noses. The smell was overpowering. Dozens of people were wearing blue coveralls and ubiquitous orange-and-yellow-crossed work vests; these workers were also wearing masks or bandanas over their faces, moving deliberately behind the half-built houses.

Gilbert and Gary exited the vehicle. The smell was so thick in the air and the despair was so thick in his heart that Gilbert's eyes were full of water and tears were spilling down his cheeks. Scraps of comments peppered with obscenities reached him from far away. Then he heard someone wailing a long, desperate cry of grief.

The white oil company trucks with their grossly ironic green logos circled the perimeter of the scene of the spill. They keep driving around and burning their money, Gilbert thought.

So this is the epicenter. Gilbert imagined a crystal vase falling onto a tile floor and smashing spectacularly. He imagined the skittering of a hundred thousand splinters of clear glass, each one containing its own tiny rainbow. He imagined bigger shards of crystal right where the vase connected with the floor. He imagined tiny specks reaching the far corners of the room, where they would remain undetected until a hapless bare foot or a child's curious hand discovered them in a sharp shock of pain. He imagined mysterious drops of blood spilling from invisible, insidious wounds.

"Half a kilometer from the river," said Gary.

"If that," said Gilbert.

The expanse of black oily crude wasn't visible from Haisla Boulevard, but the onlookers saw it in their minds as being full of rainbows. They pictured the prismatic effect of oil refracting light in its ink-black darkness. Television newscasts had been showing puddles of dark chemicals for more than a year preceding the pipeline's construction—ominous warnings from prior disasters. The oil would seep across the ground and drain into the water unstoppably. The first pictures in the media would feature these black alien puddles clogging wetlands, coating plant life, and choking out oxygen from everything stationary in their path. Within a day or two, the bird photos would begin. There would be nauseating images of unrecognizable avian life. Their feathers would be glued together with black oil. Their flight would be stolen from them probably forever. The fish would follow, washed up on gooey black banks, their gills clogged and their eyes popping with asphyxiation. And then there were the bears.

Gilbert didn't want to think about the bears.

Without warning, Peter Langston—one half of Kitimat's television news team—appeared before Gilbert, brandishing a microphone and flanked by a cameraman.

"The prediction you made before the pipeline went through has come true, Mr. Crow. Can you tell us how you feel right now?" Peter smiled brightly.

Gilbert looked through the journalist and ignored the camera, his body language indicating that he would not speak.

"Well, I guess we have our answer," said Peter. "On me," he directed. The cameraman obediently swung around and focused on the journalist.

"Early this morning a woman walking her dog noticed a strong smell of oil and alerted the Kitimat Fire Department, who came to investigate. They found a large pool of oil accumulating behind this housing development," Peter said, indicating the construction site behind him. "Officials at Elba Energy have confirmed that the pipeline they installed last year has ruptured just north of here. There is no estimate available yet as to the size of the spill. However, Elba Energy spokesperson Lily Perch says that cleanup crews have been mobilized, and they are focusing on keeping the spill from reaching the Kitimat River, which flows just one hundred meters away. The cause of the pipeline rupture is not yet known."

Gilbert's internal soundtrack to the oil spill disaster on the day it happened was the mournful chanting of his ancestors and the loud, low, sombre beat of a funeral drum. He walked along the taped-off perimeter of the tragedy breathing through a folded t-shirt. He sought a glimpse of wet, black oil the way motorists stood beside their cars gazing at highway carnage, seeking bright red blood in spite of their better instincts. Later on, long after Anne arrived and began sleeping on the couch in his cabin, she confessed over midnight coffee that her soundtrack to the spill had been classical European music: a slow string adagio building to an eventual orchestral crash of grief the moment she saw her first oil-bedraggled bird.

As if standing outside of his own body, Gilbert noted with numb curiosity his lack of anger. He supposed his anger had all been used up in the fight to prevent the pipeline from being built. The spill was inevitable, so he had been as angry as if it had already happened back when he and his fellow anti-pipeline activists were still blocking roads, hefting placards, and chaining themselves to bulldozers. He wasn't immediately moved to leap into action and help the cleanup crews. Oil spills, like big car accidents, leave massive damage and destruction in their wake. A child in the backseat who wasn't wearing a seatbelt and becomes paralyzed from the waist down after a head-on collision will need help learning to navigate life in a wheelchair. He would require psychological counselling to help him become philosophical about his new reality, but nothing would give him back the use of his legs. This pristine waterway, these precious plants and animals, the grand and glorious ecosystem Gilbert and his ancestors called home—all of this had been irrevocably tainted. To a certain extent it had been damaged beyond repair. It was a grim reality.

Perfectly formed white clouds sailed inland overhead in a field of brilliant blue. A yellow and black school bus rumbled by behind Gilbert, making its quotidian trip from bus stops to the school. A small private plane buzzed quietly in the distance. Gilbert's eyes were smarting and watering as the chemicals in the oil permeated his cells. When one of the orange-vested workers shouted in the forest, Gilbert squinted in that direction. It was then that he saw the flash of Moksgm'ol's blonde back as the bear struggled to escape.

Moksgm'ol

I wake and a vile man-smell assails my nostrils. It is a sharp, sour smell, similar to the stench of their hard-grey roadways, but it is somehow fresher. Behind the big smell, there are other smells. They are not forest, not river, not fish, not bear, not earth, and not tree. It is an assault of man-smells. I remain motionless, except for my ears, which I cock up and turn in the direction of the stink.

Men—many men—break and blunder and block one way to escape. There are other ways to escape from here, all dangerous. It was like this with men last after-warm, before-cold time in this very place. They blocked the same way to escape. Then the cold, white blanket of snow came and the men retreated. They left behind—as men typically do—an array of strange man-things. It changed the forest there in that place. The men did not return in warm-time, so I, Moksgm'ol, reclaimed this place, which was a place that I had always known.

On this morning, I must choose a different way to escape and change my sleeping place to somewhere else. The terrible smell of many men is intolerable. I begin to choose my escape, moving in a grey mistiness under a grey, cloud-strewn sky. The forest is rank with men and the wind coming inland from the salty wide water. Gusts of wind push sounds and smells toward me—at least for this moment they do. Then the wind direction changes. I must stop again and again to choose a new way.

The wind shifts again and then, impossibly, there is a man in front of me. I am on my hind legs and I roar my displeasure. Be gone man! I am Moksgm'ol! Be gone! She does not move. It is a female man. I smell her blood. I sense her menses I am Moksgm'ol! Be gone!

Running I am running crushing crashing wanting away from the man, and then there are more men. I smell a smack of stink again. I veer again away to find another way! When I come upon a line of yellow metal machines, I turn and crash.

Men are yelling behind me. They have seen Moksgm'ol. I feel their senses turned toward me. I must run.

Then the stink is all around me. I see the way to escape and I know the way, but I must run through the men's ways and the men's things. There are too many things to fight. I must use speed to break beyond the barrier that the men have made with things and smells. Not seeing anything, I am crashing around. I want only the quiet green of a man-less forest. I only want to be away from men. I only want to be somewhere that is for bears.

The Impossible

News of the pipeline rupture and the massive oil spill in Kitimat didn't reach the staff of the Churchill Northern Studies Centre until a full twenty-four hours after the accident had occurred. Anne, Jane, and Ian, who were two time zones ahead of British Columbia, woke early that day to collect field data as a team. The scientists consumed a hearty breakfast of pancakes, fruit, and maple syrup; collected their cameras, equipment, safety gear, and cold weather gear; and then struck out on foot into Wapusk National Park. The day was cold and clear. Later on, Jane noted that the exceptionally good visibility afforded by the weather conditions was a contributing factor to the record number of bears that the team sighted that day. One particularly malnourished sow had not been seen for ten weeks. The team had feared the worst. Anne was the first to spot her.

"There's Tlingit!" Anne half-yelled and half-whispered as she pressed the binoculars to her face.

"Well, I'll be darned," muttered Ian, following the line of Anne's extended arm and spotting the skinny bear.

"It's too distant for positive identification," said Jane without looking up from the notebook on which she was meticulously recording the temperature, the direction of the wind, the snow pack conditions, and the confirmed bear sightings.

Anne's contempt for Jane Minoto overwhelmed her with a sudden ferocity. She placed the lenses of her binoculars directly on Jane's face and pushed, forcing the woman's face upwards.

"Look for yourself," hissed Anne, her face turning scarlet.

"Ow. That hurt!" Jane blinked back incredulous tears.

"Hey now. Hey now," Ian appeased. "Take it easy, ladies. Anne, get a grip. Jane, have a look. I'm pretty sure Anne is right. That's Tlingit."

The sighting was confirmed, but the damage had already been done. Jane retreated to her meticulous documentation in haughty silence. Anne trudged along, heavy with remorse. The women ignored Ian's valiant attempts at levity.

"What a stunning day. This is easily the clearest, warmest day we've had since summer, wouldn't you say?" Ian stuck out his neck expectantly, hoping for an answer.

The bog underfoot had a crusty, thin top layer of ice. Their footsteps crunched with each step, the sound carrying and announcing their presence to the birds and small mammals that scattered at their approach. The bog was raised and navigable, a partly frozen table of water and vegetation providing ideal denning sites for polar bears. This was Ian's area of expertise: topographical changes caused by the increasingly warm climactic conditions. If the permafrost below the bog thawed, the bog would officially and permanently become a fen, a swampy area unsuitable for bears and people alike that was too wet to get around in without fins and gills or wings.

As the hours passed and the sun moved overhead, the trio's footsteps began to squish instead of crunch. Ian held up his hand, signalling for them to halt. The stretched smile of forced optimism he had worn all morning slid off his face.

Jane began once again to busy herself with her notebook. Ian removed his nylon zip bag from his shoulder and extracted an aluminum tripod, a survey camera, a collapsible depth-measurement stick, and a notebook. Anne couldn't suppress her grin. Ian's long, skinny limbs matched the long, skinny tools of his trade, extendable apparatuses reaching from the land to the sky.

Anne wandered away from her colleagues, scanning the horizon methodically—as she had every day here in Manitoba—for her beloved bears. Occasionally, she glanced back at Ian and tried to monitor his progress. With his face maintaining a professional blankness, Ian proceeded wordlessly with his measurements. There was no mystery, though, thought Anne. They were all here in Churchill on forgone conclusions. It's necessary to collate and tabulate the data, she thought, but the planet is warming up, which means that the polar bear's habitat is shrinking. The precise amount of prime bog real estate that had been reduced to soggy fen hardly seemed to matter. With less habitat space available for Ian to survey, there were fewer starving, homeless bears for Anne to count.

The sun scoured the landscape, merciless in the solid blue sky. Amid the insects chirping and the birds calling, melting ice created the insidious trickling sound of countless little drops. The little expedition that had been so merry in the morning was by late afternoon a grim trio. Their hair was stuck to their foreheads with sweat, and splashes of warm, wet mud stuck to their ankles and hips.

"In this generation, the meaning of good weather has changed so much," mused Anne out loud as they approached the square, geometric sprawl of the Research Centre buildings. "My grandmother would have called this a damn fine day."

Ian smiled wryly. "Should we debrief at dinner, then?"

Anne grunted her assent.

"I'll present my findings over breakfast tomorrow," said Jane. Anne was immediately inwardly pleased that she wouldn't have to deal with Jane's stilted, wooden company until the following day. Less than half an hour later, though, both women heard Ian yelling from the common room.

The three scientists were suddenly together again, standing incredulous before the Centre's lone television.

Of course, all naturalists had found the Elba Energy Company's oil pipeline from Alberta to British Columbia's Pacific coast to be abhorrent, but polar bear specialists found the proposal absolutely repellent. Kermode—or Spirit bears, the other white bears—were the most prominent creatures cited by pipeline opponents. Unique, beautiful, and existing at the top of the food chain, the spirit bears and their habitat would be harmed by an oil spill badly enough that there was no disagreement among the Friends of Bears that the pipeline was a bad idea. These very scientific minds, however, wanted to believe that modern pipeline technology was infinitely safer. They needed to believe that industry standards were more rigorous and that all interested parties had carried out the proper amount of research and development. They needed to believe that the pipeline project had been given the green light with the blessings of good science.

Yet there they were. Images were flashing on the screen. The hallmarks of environmental disaster were all in one place: the facemasks, the yellow tape, the inadequate and ill-equipped emergency vehicles, and the clusters of horrified onlookers.

Tears sprung to Anne's eyes as the impact of the news seeped into her consciousness. She glanced at her colleagues. Ian's mouth was opening and closing rhythmically and convulsively like a fish gasping for breath. Jane was inscrutable. Her mouth was a straight line and her brown eyes were dead.

Since it was breaking news, few details were available. The local reporter's zeal revealed his poorly suppressed excitement. His bushy eyebrows bounced up and down, punctuating his report. The pipeline had ruptured, causing oil to flow out into a forest that was within the municipality of Kitimat. Kitimat, he explained, was the harbour city from which massive supertankers navigated a narrow waterway through a breathtaking, awe-inspiring ecosystem. The coastal rainforest was replete with ancient trees and the symbolic, beautiful Kermode, or spirit bears.

The reporter turned his attention to an onlooker he appeared to recognize, and with a macabre half-smile he demanded to know the man's opinion. The proud, serious face of a middle-aged First Nations man filled the screen. He was handsome, thought Anne, though that wasn't a powerful enough descriptor. He was gorgeous. Black, shiny hair hung loosely around his tanned, linear face. His nose, jaw, and cheekbones were all majestic and defined.

He did not speak. He stared beyond the camera, beyond Kitimat, and beyond the clouds. His black eyes seemed to stare beyond the veil that separates the living from the dead. He stared right into Anne's soul and told her something. His stare travelled from northern British Columbia on Canada's West coast all the way to the shores of Hudson Bay in central

Canada, in Manitoba, where it found Anne McCraig. His stare went inside of her, where it found her bloodstream and then circulated throughout her body until it found the part of her that was connected to the bears. He then told her about the part of him that belonged to the bears.

He never said a word. The reporter called him Mister Crow.

Jonathan Fuhrenmann

He began packing to go up north and help with the cleanup the very day that he heard about the spill. His rent was paid up for the month of September for the house he shared on East 12th Street in Vancouver with four other young people. He had no pets and no kids, so there were no other arrangements to be made. It was raining in Vancouver and the video clips of Kitimat showed mainly clear skies. He was close to his monthly quota soliciting advertisers for *The Georgia Straight*, a popular urban entertainment weekly. It wasn't, in any case, the pinnacle of his career ambitions.

Jonathan cared about the environment, just like a growing percentage of young people did. He reduced, reused, and recycled. Since he typically rode a bicycle and took public transportation, he would have to ensure that his mother wasn't presently driving the Volvo wagon so that he could make the eight-hundred-kilometer road trip up to Kitimat. He looked the part as well, with his long, lanky hair, his casual clothes, and the Haida-inspired tattoo on his right forearm. He was picking away at college courses, supplementing his geography degree by specializing in environmental sustainability. He thought about his great-grandfather a lot.

Many young people cared deeply about the planet: its forests, its oceans, its endangered species, the breathability of the air, and the prudent and sustainable use of its natural resources. The issues were pressing, and the need for change was immediate. One didn't need a Nazi-sympathizing, panda-abusing right-wing bastard of an ancestor to galvanize one's determination. Jonathan had that extra edge.

We learn about our ancestors gradually through photo-album snippets and dinner-table anecdotes repeated and expanded over the years. When Jonathan was a young boy, he saw pictures of his great-grandfather, Lothar, in the same frame as a large, live panda bear. His childish impression was one of benevolence. Great-grandpa liked animals, he had thought. Jonathan's family had lived and worked in and around Cologne, Germany, for centuries. In the basement den, his parents displayed memorabilia from the Kolner Zoo in Cologne. There was a framed map and prints of posters advertising various special exhibits: African Safari at the Kolner Zoo, Underwater Adventure at the Kolner Zoo, and Happy the Giant Panda at the Kolner Zoo. The last poster depicted his great-grandfather's smiling visage.

At eleven years old, Jonathan had learned about the Holocaust from his parents, who held a liberal, no-excuses perspective. His parents were not deniers but since he was young and impressionable, they had minimized the Holocaust to a degree—not the reality of it or the horror, but the family's involvement in it.

Jonathan himself had done his own share of fabricating, extemporizing, and imagining what his ancestors had been like in Nazi Germany. Lothar, he decided early on, had immersed himself in the animal kingdom in order to push away the grim political reality of his nation and his nationality. He had spent his days promoting his animal exhibits, and acquiring and caring for exotic creatures. His wife, Greta, would have done the same thing. She would have kept the home fires burning. She would have put the schnitzel on the table. She would have laundered the white shirts—white, not brown—pressing and hanging them with characteristic German precision in Lothar's armoire. He was fifteen and lurking at the perimeter of one of his parents' prolonged, wine-infused dinner parties when he first heard about the human exhibits. His father had made some reference to Asian drivers in Vancouver, a stereotype that was not uncommon.

"Careful, Bernie," his mother had slurred. "Your heritage is racist. Steer clear of those comments!"

"It's not racist; it's observable fact," his father had answered.

"Bernie's great-grandfather put people in zoos," his mother offered up to the general conversation.

"What do you mean he put them in zoos?" one guest asked.

"He held human exhibits. He got a hold of some native people, dressed them up in feathers and rawhide, and charged admission!"

"It was a common occurrence at the time, Hilary."

"So was genocide."

Jonathan had retreated as the argument escalated. The next morning, his mother—her face a mask of chalk and her hands shaking beside her coffee—regarded him with the mute resentment of the seriously hung over as he scrambled eggs, drank a carton of milk, and whistled the melody of his current favourite song. He ignored all of the warning signs of his mother's poisonous mood.

"Did Great-granddad really put people in zoos?"

"Oh, for Christ's sake."

"Well, did he?"

She sighed, hung her head, and looked up at him from puffy eyes. "Yes, he did. He was a Nazi sympathizer. He was an opportunist. He gauged the public sentiment and gambled that they would pay to see brown-skinned people behind bars."

"Wow. That sucks," the teenage Jonathan had answered.

Jonathan asked a lot of questions over the next week, growing increasingly despondent with the answers he received. He began to investigate tentatively on the internet, which led him rapidly to the Allied Forces' fire bombing of Cologne on the thirtieth and the thirty-first of May 1942. It had—miraculously in Jonathan's opinion—never been discussed in his presence. The thousand-bomber raid—codenamed Operation Millennium—was intended to have results that were devastating enough to damage German morale or potentially smack Germany right out of the war. The firebombing resulted in just short of five hundred deaths. Over five thousand people were injured and over twelve thousand buildings were damaged or severely destroyed.

Bernard Fuhrenmann was visibly uncomfortable with his son's research, but he had nothing to add to the facts that his son presented to him at regular intervals. Often, he wouldn't even deign to lower the newspaper that was blocking his face to deliver his curt replies.

"What happened to the animals?" asked Jonathan one day.

Bernard slowly lowered the newspaper and regarded his son expressionlessly.

"What animals?"

"The animals in the Kolner zoo. What happened to them?"

Bernard momentarily furrowed his brow and then answered flatly, "They died, I expect."

"Didn't anyone try to save them?" spat Jonathan.

"The city was on fire, Jonathan. There were human lives to save. I don't suppose that anything could have been done about the animals." The newspaper then ascended once more.

With fire raining like an apocalypse from the sky without precedent or explanation, the animals must have been terrified, their situation all the more gruesome and horrible because of their captivity. There was nowhere to run and nowhere to hide. The humans had the context of the war and the knowledge that their nation was besieged and that attacks were likely. There must have been sirens wailing at the sound of the approaching enemy airplanes. The people of Cologne could have tried to run for shelter in basements or flee the city in vehicles.

Jonathan tried to imagine his great-grandfather that night. Lothar Fuhrenmann, heroically running from cage to cage with a great ring of skeleton keys in his hand, yanking open barred enclosures and calling to the animals, encouraging them to run for their lives. What had actually happened? Jonathan's intuition told him that what had actually happened was something wrong, something shameful.

Dawn was approaching on the thirty-first of May, 1942. There were no witnesses in the Kolner Zoo, Lothar Fuhrenmann was the only human soul on the premises. The enclosures were barely visible through the smoke, though the skies all around glowed orange and red. With the sounds of crashes, sirens, and screams, Cologne was a cacophony of cataclysm. Lothar strode directly to Happy's cage. The bear was pacing and whimpering pathetically. Lothar fingered the irregular edges of two objects in his front trouser pocket: a metal key and a loaded handgun. When Happy saw him the bear became much more agitated, swaying frantically at the door of his enclosure. His red-rimmed eyes were exploding from their sockets. Lothar came to a stop and leaned toward the animal with clenched fists and teeth. "Fuck you, you fucking Chinese pig-bear," Lothar hissed. "Useless fucking waste of time and money. Thanks for nothing. I hope you enjoy your incineration as much as you have enjoyed your incarceration." Having made his decision, Lothar wheeled around and ran for his life.

A new version of his heritage descended on Jonathan and enveloped him, scratchy and uncomfortable as a hair shirt. Goodbye bratwurst and black forest cake. Goodbye Hansel and Gretel. Hello brown shirts, barricades, cattle cars, crying children, and firing squads.

Lothar Fuhrenmann

Cringing in the crawl space under the house, Lothar and his family survived the firebombing of Cologne, although their home did not. They were obligated to listen to the screams for help without responding. They had to listen to the dire rumbling, the crashing of collapsing buildings, and the wailing of countless sirens. They were all held captive within the loud silence that Herr Fuhrenmann had imposed. Greta kept her children drawn to her ample bosom, a tousled little blonde head under each arm. Dust and tiny rocks disgorged from above them, dirtying their hair, clothes, and skin, and sticking to the tracks of tears on the cheeks of Frau Fuhrenmann and her babies.

Lothar's cringing white face was set in a fierce, triumphant grimace. "Schweigen," he would bark at the tiniest whimper from his wife or children. *Shut up,* he thinks. *Shut up and take what's coming.*

I will begin again after tonight, he thought. There would be no more zoos, animals, shit, straw, feathers, or fur. There would be no more courting the public, that horrible bitch. There would be no more trying to separate the ignorant masses from their money. He would walk out of this country a refugee and start again. He would go to Canada, hack an existence out of the wilderness, and farm the way his ancestors had. Greta and his children could follow him if they wished to. He wouldn't shirk his duties as a man and a father.

Morning arrived in an eerie silence. The children and Greta were asleep, propped up in a corner of the crawl space under a layer of filth. Lothar kicked the heavy slatted wooden door open, revealing a grey expanse of ash, smoke, and dust. The streets were unrecognizable, littered with bodies and burnt debris. Lothar picked his way through what was left of Cologne, surveying the death and destruction with satisfaction, and circuitously made his way to the zoo to inspect his investments. If any of those stupid, godforsaken beasts are left alive, he thought, I'll sell them for seed money to start my new life. He was not afraid of the big feline predators—lions, tigers, panthers, and mountain lions—running wild, free of their bombed and demolished cages; he had no fear because he himself had put bullets in their skulls the night before.

Lothar knew why he hadn't shown Happy the same mercy. That big dumb panda had caused him so much trouble. That Chinese bear had cost him so much money, giving back little for all of the trouble it had taken to feed and house it. Lothar wanted the black and white beast to suffer.

The Kolner Zoo was a mess. There were blackened craters where cages used to be. No longer vertical, the twisted metal bars curved and pointed in odd directions. He could hear unidentified animals squeaking for help, but he didn't follow up on the sounds. He made his way to Happy's enclosure.

At first he was certain that Happy the Panda was dead. The enclosure couldn't have been compromised, he thought, because the bear was there. There was a mound of matted black and white fur lying in a great lump. It must have died of a heart attack probably, thought Lothar. Or maybe shrapnel had struck it. But then the animal moved. Happy, perhaps detecting the presence of another sentient being, rolled up into a sitting position. He stared bleary-eyed through air thick with destruction at the angry, skinny man. To Lothar, the stunned panda bear looked unsurprised, nonplussed, and unimpressed. He looked impudent.

"Gott verdammt," breathed Lothar. "You lived. You lived, you big, stupid, lucky animal."

Lothar reached into the left breast pocket of his zoo uniform. He had not removed the uniform since the bombing had begun the previous day. Yes, there it was, the paper with the American telephone number scrawled on it. "Anthony Ferguson, Saint Louis Zoo" was printed underneath the number in Lothar's own handwriting. Ferguson, the purchaser for the Saint Louis, Missouri Zoo, was a damn cheapskate—at least, he had been up until that point. And up until that day, the money would have had to pass through all of the correct channels. The paperwork would have had to be completed to everyone's specifications. Who was there to watch now, thought Lothar. All of the money could be deposited directly into Lothar's personal account. He needed to get to a telephone. That was his task for the day.

A long, strangled cry pierced the air in what was left of the Kolner Zoo. Maybe it's a peacock, thought Lothar absently. He looked around at the rubble that used to be the zoo and once again he was filled with a certain satisfaction. It was a definite end to this miserable chapter of his life.

"Make me some money," Lothar hissed to Happy before leaving to find a telephone.

Yukuai

he combined scat of a multitude of animals—I smell it every morning, so before opening my tired eyes I know that everything is the same. I am still a prisoner, I am still not free and I must wonder if I ever was or if that was all a dream.

The hard grey pool of fetid water is dotted with brown leaves this morning. It is not the same as yesterday. I will investigate. I roll onto my paws and stretch widely. I smell the grass that I slept on. Naturally I want to hide my scent, but there is nowhere to hide. Every day there are many things like this that I want to do, but they are all futile or impossible. These urges are what make me believe that the dream must have been real. Why would I want to hide where I sleep? Why would I want to hide where I scat? Why would I want to hide from the men and their young, who stand and stink and point and talk all day, unless at some time it had been possible to do so?

The rolling object with the man-who-brings-bamboo arrives, noisy and smelling terrible. But at least there will be bamboo. He stops his object and takes the bamboo from it. For some reason I cannot fathom he stands and speaks and speaks instead of throwing in the bamboo. He makes his man-noises and points into my prison like all of the other men who come here throughout the day. I like different things if they are pleasant, but this isn't pleasant. I want him to throw in the bamboo without speaking as he does every day. Finally, he throws the bamboo into my enclosure, gets back into his loud and smelly object, and rolls away.

The speaking is not good. The speaking reminds me of another man, another prison, and another night long ago. It was the fire-night, and the man was the cruel man who sometimes spat his foul spit toward me through the bars. I do not understand men's words when they speak, but I can intuit if they feel love or hatred. I know the difference between the child who speaks in gentle tones of wonder and the child who makes sure that no one is watching when he throws a rock.

The foul, spitting man was full of hatred. He would have killed me if he could have.

Gilbert

Walking home, the smells and the noises receded. Many cars slowed beside him. Some people spoke to him or called his name, including Gary in his beat up white truck. Gilbert did not acknowledge them. Walking away I am walking away I am walking, walking, walking, he thought. He kept his eyes straight ahead, but he focused on nothing.

He arrived home, left his shoes on the porch, and went inside, closing the door gingerly behind him. He went into his bedroom, stretched out in the exact centre of his bed, crossed his arms over his chest, and stared at the irregularities in the ceiling. He had assumed this meditative, supine position in this exact location many times over the years, often missing Clara and trying to conjure her presence beside him in the bed that they used to share. Every tiny fissure of the ceiling was familiar to him—every bump, every crack, and every discoloration. His eyes wandered over the topography of sorrow above him. His mind was numb.

The days and nights that he had spent heating the mental forge and hammering out solutions were now over. There was no more fuel for the fire that had roared beneath Gilbert's passion. Gilbert had tried to save Clara's life and halt the construction of the pipeline. He had tried and failed over and over. Gilbert had worked for a tree planting company many years ago. He remembered the feeling of nobility he had had about this job, he remembered feeling like a steward of the land. Then one day a white man had told him the story of Sisyphus, who was condemned to roll a rock up a hill eternally only to have it roll back down over and over until the end of time.

"Sisyphus would be a great name for a tree planting company!" the man had laughed. "Plant and plant and plant and plant and watch them getting cut down or being browsed by deer or succumbing to an insect infestation. Look! You can see the whole cycle from here."

Gilbert had stopped and leaned onto his shovel. He had seen that it was true. Machinery was buzzing and smashing on a distant hillside, clear-cutting the virgin forest and removing every stick. Rough roads zigzagged across a brown, uneven devastation. The surrounding hills were a patchwork of forests in various stages of growth and decay. There was a yellow triangle where a plantation was failing, and a pale green rectangle of a young successful stand of trees. He and the other tree planters only had to look up to see what would become of the fragile seedlings nestled in the bags at their waists. The young trees were destined to be felled, to become particleboard and toilet paper. With the evidence of this process all around him, Gilbert felt not the nobility of tree planting, but the futility of it. It had reminded him of another story, which he told to his companion.

The Great Bear Punishes People

The Great Bear heard the crying of her creatures and she went to investigate. The people she had created from brown bear cubs now had the intelligence and cunning she had given them to survive. Even so, they were immature. They needed skins for clothing, trees for fuel and housing, feathers for decoration, and stones for weapons, and they took all of these things wastefully and thoughtlessly. They left animals slaughtered and stripped of their skins, and they left the rest of their bodies to decay. There were more than enough bodies for Crow and Raven, the carrion eaters, to find and use for nourishment. The people felled trees and carved their trunks into canoes. They left branches to suffocate the forest floor. They shot birds with arrows; the birds toppled from the sky only to have the largest of their feathers yanked roughly from their bodies. The remains of the birds were left to wilt and waste. Even the stone chipped for arrowheads had been stolen disrespectfully from Snake's warming spot and the mouths of Fish's rivers.

The Great Bear began by warning the people about their wastefulness. She then sent them droughts and floods. She diverted the herds and flocks, and she caused sparks to fly when stones were harvested, which lead to widespread fires burning down villages, forests, and fields. Still, the people did not learn. Whenever the herds and flocks returned or the forests grew back, the humans wastefully used up their precious gifts. The Great Bear saw that people would destroy everything that she had created unless she taught them a long, hard lesson.

The Great Bear thickened the coats of all of the bears. Then she focused her breath on the frozen place of the White Bears, blowing cold wind, ice, and snow across the world. She blew until the world was covered with ice. Many of the people did not survive, but the Great Bear watched carefully and ensured that some of them did survive. Then, slowly and gradually, the Great Bear warmed the world with warm breath from her body, and the people were grateful. They learned this time to use every part of every animal they sacrificed, and every twig and branch of every tree that they chopped down. They even gave thanks for the rocks that they chipped, as they knew that ice might cover them and make them unreachable.

In the northern night sky, the faint constellation known as Lynx represents the Great Bear's long, cold breaths, which blew across the world and made it cold for a long time. Lynx is located directly overhead during the winter months to remind people that although the world is cold for only a few months, the coldness might return to stay for a hundred years or more if they become wasteful or careless with animals and plants ever again.

Gilbert thought of this story again. He remembered the wise, lined face of the elder who had told him the story, firelight and smoke wreathing her visage. Her voice had rung with prophetic conviction. He thought about how the Great Bear would surely punish people again for their wastefulness. His eyes widened as he thought about global warming: the punishment had already begun. A terribly symmetrical natural disaster was warming the planet up instead of cooling it off. The ice caps were melting, ocean levels were rising, major cities were flooding, crops were failing, and babies and the elderly were succumbing to heat. He was struck by a feeling of powerlessness and inevitability. People needed to learn a lesson. They would keep on extracting their oil, driving their cars, flying their planes, and running their factories until the world was a parched, arid, and hostile place. Only then would they learn their lesson and give thanks for every drop of rain that fell and every calorie of energy that gave them the energy to transport themselves across modest and moderate distances. He thought about Max and Charlotte. He thought about his grandson Jack and the imminent arrival of his newest grandchild. Things would only get worse for them. Gilbert looked at the cracks and pits on his ceiling for a long time. He considered the imperfections overhead until he descended into a deep, troubled sleep.

Anne McCraig

I t was easy to find out who Gilbert Crow was and where he lived. A quick internet search of oil pipeline protests in and around Kitimat elicited dozens of hits, including the man's name. Leaving the Churchill Research Centre for an indeterminate period of time right in the middle of her residency proved to be a trickier task. Ian and Jane offered plenty of reasons why she shouldn't go to Kitimat, but none of them changed Anne's determination. She took her leave of absence, packed her bags, purchased her tickets, and then departed.

Anne arrived in Kitimat four days after the spill was discovered. The little plane circled a flat, green valley surrounded by dramatic snow-capped peaks. To the west she spied the great expanse of the Pacific Ocean spreading out across the horizon. Channels to the ocean spread out from Kitimat in a network, great arteries dividing into veins and capillaries. The islands were like organs in a big green-and-blue body. When Anne descended the aluminum steps of a small plane and stepped onto a remote tarmac, she was immediately overwhelmed by the odour of residual airplane exhaust. For one crazy moment, she thought she smelled oil from the accident, but then she shook her head. Kitimat was fifty-six kilometers to the south. As she stepped out of the tiny Northwest Regional Airport and walked toward the lone waiting taxi, though, Anne couldn't rid her nostrils of the stench of gasoline and chemicals. She frowned at the insidious irony of all of the fossil fuel that had been used to facilitate her trip to this place.

The First Nations cab driver said his name was Little Ted, and Anne suppressed a giggle. Tall and corpulent, he dwarfed the taxi that he was leaning against. He had thick eyeglasses that sat slightly askew on the bridge of his broad nose. He tossed her heavy bags into the trunk with a nonchalance that indicated his great strength.

"Where to?" asked Little Ted. "The spill?"

Anne was startled. "Well, not directly." she muttered.

"Hotel or motel then? There aren't many of them, but you can probably still get a room."

"I..."Anne hesitated for a moment before blurting out, "Do you know Gilbert Crow?"

There was a long pause. Little Ted tilted his head to consider her in the rear-view mirror. He pushed his spectacles up with a finger and then spoke slowly and deliberately. "There are just over eight thousand people in Kitimat and I'm one of three cab drivers. I know just about everybody. Do *you* know Gilbert Crow?"

"Well, um, no—not exactly. I *feel* that I know him, though," Anne answered. To her amazement, Little Ted didn't laugh.

"You feel you know Gilbert. Well, maybe you can help him out then," said Little Ted.

As the half-hour drive began, Little Ted gave Anne a synopsis of what the past two years in Kitimat had been like. He told her about the protests, the highway block-ades, the media coverage, and the controversy. For every activist who cited the spectre of environmental disaster in their determination to prevent the construction of the pipeline, said Little Ted, there was a businessperson touting the economic potential and benefits of the same project. Families were fractured. Children had turned against their parents.

"But not the Crow family," said Little Ted. "Max and Charlotte stood with their father. Max thought that the pipe-line was a good thing, but he never said a word. He supported his dad anyway. They had just lost their mother—Clara, Gilbert's wife—when the pipeline project was announced. Gilbert and Charlotte Crow fought the oil company like it could bring their mother—their Clara—back. They fought it with their grief. Gilbert's friends—and I put myself in this category—were worried that his grief would come if the pipe-line proposal succeeded. Well, yeah, it did. Elba Energy built the damn thing. But Gilbert—he was okay. Disappointed, yeah, but okay." Little Ted fell silent.

"What's your story?" he asked finally. "You a reporter?"

"Hardly," Anne answered. "I'm a biologist. I've been studying polar bears in Churchill, Manitoba."

"So, you came because of the spirit bear?"

"No," Anne answered. "Well, not exactly. I don't know precisely why I've come here. I just need to make a difference right now—somehow. I can't do anything for the polar bears. It's terrible to feel such helplessness. The ice keeps melting, the bears keep suffering, and I keep, well, gaining weight." Unexpected tears sprang to Anne's eyes. "I don't know why I just said that. I'm sorry. Please excuse me." She wiped her face with her sleeve and looked out the window.

Little Ted drove quietly, stealing surreptitious glances at Anne in his rear-view mirror from time to time. He thought that she was a healthy, red-cheeked woman with sparkling eyes, a ready smile, and a tender heart. Little Ted drove to Gilbert Crow's cabin.

Anne said nothing as the cabbie drove through the center of Kitimat, past a smattering of hotels and onto a quiet residential street. It came to a stop in front of a modest A-frame cabin. He manoeuvred his bulk out of the driver's seat and lumbered around the back, where he opened the trunk, removed her bags, and then carried them over to the wooden porch. She got out of the cab and followed him tentatively, stopping halfway across the scrubby yard.

"Umm, excuse me, but this doesn't..." Anne began. Having conversed with Little Ted for an hour, she didn't consider him to be mentally defective or incompetent in any way. He had, however, clearly forgotten exactly whom she was and where she wished to go. "I was thinking a hotel would be better. I don't live here." But Little Ted was rapping firmly on the door of the cabin.

There was no answer and no movement from inside the cabin. The big man turned to face her. "He's not getting up. We're going to have to just do it," said Little Ted, as if the plan that was fully formed in his brain had been worked out with Anne. Little Ted opened the front door and walked inside, beckoning for Anne to follow him.

"Hey Gil. Yeah, it's Little Ted. You there?" Little Ted waited for a moment and then shouted, "Gilbert! You've got a visitor. She's from Churchill, Manitoba, man."

There was no response. Anne stood on the threshold of the cabin feeling a little panicky and looking back and forth between her bags and the interior of this stranger's home. It was tidy but comfortable, she thought. Family photographs hung on the walls, as well as several striking paintings in the style of the Pacific Northwest First Nations. Colourful blankets had been folded neatly over the armchair and the couch. A mask in the kitchen area supervised the cooking and the eating with a stretched-out grin and huge, staring eyes. "Listen, I..." she began to say.

Little Ted walked back to Anne and leaned his large, tousled head toward her blonde curls. He pushed his glasses up, but they immediately slid back down the sweaty ramp of his nose.

"Gilbert Crow hasn't spoken a word in four days. I don't think he's eaten either. My thoughts are that there's a lot of grieving he never got around to and he's doing it now. His kids have been around, but Max is pretty busy at work and Charlotte's got a baby due anytime now. She's gone to a friend's place in Terrace until this place stops reeking. A few rooms are maybe still available for rent but they won't be for long. You can sleep on Gilbert's couch and free a motel room up for someone else to come help with the cleanup. Your guts are telling you that you know Gilbert, and gut feelings are usually correct. He's a good man. You're safe here, and you can do something right away."

Little Ted reached his huge paw into the breast pocket of his plaid shirt and pulled out a business card. He handed it to Anne and said, "If you need a ride any time, call me. There's food in the fridge—Max brought it—and fish in the freezer. Gilbert likes coffee in the morning and tea for the rest of the day."

Anne allowed herself to be gently guided to a beige, over-stuffed couch. It could double as a bed, she thought, as Little Ted brought her bags inside. Little Ted indicated a door beside the little kitchen, nodding meaningfully. He opened it and spoke to the occupant in a loud, bright voice.

"You've got a house guest now, Gil. Her name is Anne, and she's here to help clean up the spill. There's no room down-town, so she's going to stay here. I'll stop by later to see how you're both getting on." Little Ted drew his bulk out of the doorframe and walked past Anne. He stopped as he exited the cabin and turned once more. "Maybe you could make him a cup of tea and a sandwich right away before he forgets that you're here." The huge taxi driver winked and smiled, and then he was gone.

Jonathan Fuhrenmann

"Land of the silver birch, home of the beaver," sang Jonathan, speeding northwest on British Columbia's Highway16 toward Kitimat. "Where still the mighty moose wander at will!" The windows were down on the old blue wagon, and a pile of camping gear obscured the rear-view mirror. "Blue lake and rocky shore, I will return once more." Jonathan's tuneful voice built to a roadworthy crescendo. "Boom diddy ah da, boom diddy ah da, boom diddy ah da, boom!" He then sang a series of love songs—not to anyone in particular but to an amorphous lover of the future—his voice warbling with earnest sentiment. He had just refuelled in Smithers. It was ten o'clock in the morning on his second day of driving. He was hoping to reach Kitimat well before nightfall to find a decent, free camping spot. He had brought with him a cooler full of fruit and cheese, a couple of bags of dry goods, his parents' tent, a camp stove, two sleeping bags, and an air mattress. He also had lots of black clothes. In the spirit of youthful poverty, he had canvassed his friends for any extra black clothes they owned. Oil stains wouldn't show up on black.

The spill had happened exactly where everyone had feared it would, bleeding right into the pristine waters around Kitimat. Everyone was horrified. Some people were depressed and some outraged. Jonathan imagined that many people were also indifferent. He knew there were bloodsucking corporate bastards out there who included environmental disasters like this one in the cost of doing business. These disasters made people numb. The first sizable spills were big news, but now everyone was becoming inured to images of oily birds and scummy water. The last massive spill, which was down in the Gulf of Mexico, had sickened the world. There had been an underwater explosion, and a pipe that couldn't be capped had spewed oil into the fish-rich waters off Louisiana. Days had passed and technology had failed until one couldn't even watch the news anymore. You had to look away.

Jonathan wondered about his own buoyant mood. This disaster was the very thing that he had resisted, protested, written letters against, and discussed at length in tutorials at his college. Instead of driving toward the scene of a sickening environmental crime, though, he felt like he was racing toward opportunity. People would need solutions and expertise, and here he was: Jonathan Fuhrenmann, B.Sc. He had his newly minted degree in environmental sustainability all shiny and ready for use.

Also, he was feeling the high of the road trip, which was proving to be spectacular. The highway veered west and then south again. Everywhere around him, jagged black mountain peaks were streaked with brilliant patches of snow, and every turn brought something sudden and beautiful: a little gem of a lake, a stand of imposing trees, or a meadow of late-blooming wildflowers.

"Intense," exclaimed Jonathan. It became the mantra for his trip. "In. Tense. Intense. Whoa, man, this is just in-fucking-tense!"

Just as Jonathan had hoped it would be, it was midafternoon when the blue station wagon rolled into downtown Kitimat with the windows down and the music blasting. His stringy hair was sucked sideways and flapping outside the car. Brilliant sunshine had kept his mood aloft, and his bright blue eyes were wide. A hopeful, crooked smile played on his lips. The epicenter of the oil spill wasn't difficult to locate. He didn't even have to consult his map. A long line of vehicles, including two fire trucks and several Elba Energy trucks, bordered a forested area that was demarcated with yellow tape screaming: caution. Dozens of people—some of them wearing full hazmat suits—were visibly moving in behind the trees. Jonathan parked, switched his leather sandals for rubber boots, and strode into the fray.

The reek hit him immediately. His eyes began watering and his lungs began to burn. He squinted toward the workers in the trees, who were all wearing masks of one kind or another over their mouths and noses. Disconcerted with his lack of foresight, Jonathan returned to his car, extracted a crumpled blue bandana, and fashioned a cover for his face. He knew that it would be inadequate, but after driving for two days he was determined to see the spill. He ducked under the yellow tape and made his way toward a knot of people who were struggling with shovels and buckets.

He felt a squishing sensation underfoot. Jonathan looked down at the forest floor as he walked and then at his footsteps behind him. Everything was shiny and black. The whole area was saturated with oil at the ground level. He approached the workers. They were immersing their shovels down into the top layer of vegetation, scooping up crude oil, and depositing it in buckets at a rate of two or three cups per shovelful. The method seemed futile.

"Hey man," Jonathan interrupted. "That isn't going to get all the oil up, is it?"

The woman he had addressed looked up. Her black hair was streaked with grey, and her face was lined and grimy.

"Have you registered yourself?" she asked disdainfully.

"Uh, no, man. I, like, just got here," said Jonathan.

"White tent near the fire engines." She indicated where the tent was with her gloved, oily hand. "They'll explain everything to you there."

As he approached the tent, Jonathan saw that it was flanked by four burly police officers. They all appraised him carefully as he passed.

Inside the tent, the emergency effort was briskly efficient. Jonathan presented himself at the first wooden folding table, where a woman wrote down his name, his driver's license number, and his social insurance number.

"Okay. Do you want to work with boom setting, forest skimming, dispersant application, or operating the fire hose?" she asked.

"Umm," said Jonathan. "What do they entail?"

The woman sighed. "Booms need to be secured on the river. They isolate the oil to one spot so it can be vacuumed up. There's got to be a whole series of them between here and the wharf. That's the cleanest job. Fire hoses are used for pressure dispersing the oil that's on the riverbanks. You need to be strong because the pressure is intense. The fire department will show you how to use the water pressure to move the oil once you get there. With forest skimming you immerse a shovel into the puddles on the surface and scoop it into buckets. With chemical dispersants, you need to wear a full hazmat suit and get an hour of training in the tent behind this one." She waited for him to decide.

"Uh, boom setting," said Jonathan, feeling craven but wanting to be part of oil collection out on the water.

"Okay. You'll still need a regulation mask, a suit, and some gloves. You can sign all three out from the tables behind me. Sign in and out over there," she said, indicating another table. "Every day you work. Return any equipment on your last day of work so that you don't get billed for it. Okay?"

"Yeah, okay. I'll come get that stuff tomorrow," said Jonathan. "Uh, I have to find a camping spot today. Do you know where I can camp?"

"You're on your own," said the woman. "I'm not from here. I'm just here to help with the spill." She looked over his shoulder. Two new volunteers were waiting behind him to sign up and choose their work assignments.

Jonathan stepped aside. He retreated to his car, blinking rapidly. The grim reality of the spill had taken his buoyant mood down a notch or two, he admitted to himself. That smell was horrible. He somehow hadn't anticipated the terrible omnipresence of it. He would feel better once he got to work setting booms on the water the next day. Before setting out to find a camping spot, he realized that he had another problem. The soles of his rubber boots were coated with smears of viscous oil; they would taint and stain anything they came into contact with. He removed them and rooted around in his vehicle for a plastic bag. He found one and stuffed the boots into it. He then placed the bag in the back seat of the Volvo.

As he drove back the way he had come, looking for a promising side street or a logging road, he realized that the smell of oil was permeating the vehicle. The plastic bag was doing nothing to contain it. The fumes were toxic and he could barely drive. He rolled down all of the windows. Indignation rose within him. The pipeline was repugnant hypothetically. In real life, it was heinous. It was an unpardonable crime.

Perhaps through his own attempts to be witty by describing oil as "compressed dinosaur" Jonathan had rendered the stuff less toxic and harmful in its crude state. But here it was, poisoning not just land and water but the very air that he was breathing.

Later on, lying in his hospital bed, Jonathan would reflect on this moment. He would reflect on how disconcerted he had been by the odour in his car and how full of determination and impatience he had been. A dirt road sliced off the highway at an angle on his right. He swerved onto it and followed it until he found a wide section of road. Here he parked, got out of the vehicle, and plunged into the forest. Barely twenty steps from the road he found a flattish clearing. By nightfall, Jonathan was climbing into a cosy cocoon of sleeping bags inside the jaunty electric blue dome tent, his belly full of boiled veggie dogs, apples, and whole wheat bread. By nightfall he had already trampled out a pathway between the road and his new rugged domain. He had stashed the bag with his boots in it fifty paces away from the car—safely out of smelling range. As he fell asleep, he thought about his father and his family camping trips. He thought how proud the old man would be about the order his son had imposed onto the chaos of this unknown wilderness.

The snuffling and snorting began in his unconscious. In his dream, Jonathan was carrying buckets of scraps and slop to various hungry livestock in a farmyard. He was wearing shiny, black rubber boots—not the green-with-yellow-trim pair that he actually owned. He fed a black-and-white Holstein cow that was mooing gently. He fed some chickens grain that appeared magically in the pockets of the denim overalls he was wearing. The chickens clucked and pecked cheerfully around him. He fed a donkey. The beast looked at him gratefully with big, brown, heavily lashed eyes. The pig still needed to be fed, though. It was a bright pink pig with a perfectly curled tail. Cartoon-like, it was as perfect as a pig on Old MacDonald's farm. It kept hungrily making sounds with its nose and wet tongue. In this dream, he searched behind a yellow haystack inside a red-and-white barn. The pig was nowhere to be found, but its snorting and heavy breathing were growing inexplicably louder.

A sudden heavy nudge woke Jonathan, as though he had been snoring and a bed mate had found it offensive. It took Jonathan several weighty seconds to assimilate the monster sounds of fangs and drool. The pig was outside the tent and it wanted to get in. The pig was really a bear. The bear was big. Terror descended on him.

Immobile, Jonathan continued lying there stiffly as the bear continued to circle the tent. He heard a metallic crunch. He could picture the bear as it investigated the dried remnants of soy products clinging to the sides the camp stove. He heard another crunching sound and the rake of beast's claws on manmade things. Jonathan had stashed the cooler in his car before retiring, and no other food waste was around the tent. He had flung the water in which he had boiled the veggie dogs into the undergrowth. Damn. Fuck. He strained his eyes, trying to see through the thin nylon in the thinnest of cold dawn light. He kept hearing snuffling, licking, and heavy crushing sounds.

Everything else happened so suddenly that he didn't piece it together until days later. The tent collapsed at its entrance, pushed in and down as though a great tree had fallen on it. He felt a pain in his left leg and he bit down on the zipper of his sleeping bag to remain silent. The bear tore the smooth blue fabric into ragged ribbons with its claws.

A huge hairy head exploded into his little dome. His arms scrabbled at his sides as he tried to back away from the massive presence before him, but the bear was standing on his leg. All of the advice about bear attacks he had ever known flashed inside his skull, but one thing was shouting louder than the rest, bold and in all caps: PLAY DEAD.

For the rest of his days, when Jonathan told the story, this was how it went: "Then I played dead. I mean, what else could I do? I had five hundred pounds of bear on my leg!" The truth, which he never admitted to anyone, was that he had either half-fainted or gone into a state of catatonic shock. The great drooling jaws had closed onto his left ankle, and a new flash of pain had burst in his right thigh as the animal pulled him free of the wreckage of the tent.

Enough morning light filtered through the forest for Jonathan to get a solid impression of the size of his attacker. It was the biggest bear he had ever seen, and it wasn't black but a cinnamon brown. The bear had pulled him free of the tent, but it was distracted by something above it back in the direction of the road. Later, Jonathan would have vague memories of an engine sound and men's voices. Three forestry workers had inadvertently saved Jonathan's life by stopping their truck next to Jonathan's Volvo and noisily urinating into the roadside shrubs.

The bear stood up at the sound of the car and men, towering above Jonathan. The power and the glory of the animal were overwhelming. It had a terribly bestial beauty.

Then its forelegs crashed to the ground as it turned and retreated into the forest. In this brief moment, Jonathan saw his attacker in profile. He saw the unmistakeable hump of the creature's upper back. It was a grizzly.

The Great Bear Creates Grizzlies

The Great Bear was resting among the stars. She had created the bears, the people, and the creatures of the earth, and she was pleased. She had not rested for very long, however, when she heard something squalling and squawking below her.

The Brown Bears of the earth ate well. They harvested berries and nuts, and they ate the fat pink flesh of salmon. They drank clear cold water from the rivers and streams. They were so healthy that their cubs grew bigger and stronger with each generation. One spring, all of the mother brown bears gave birth to cubs that were much bigger and stronger than previous brown bears. These cubs quickly realized the advantages of their strength, and they began to bully their own parents, brothers, sisters, and elders.

The salmon run arrived in a great flush of red fish. The big, bullying bears wouldn't let any of the others near the riverbanks. The berries turned purple and ripe on the shiny green bushes. The bully bears ate all of the fruit themselves. They wouldn't let any of the others get near the fruit. Naturally, the bears began to argue and fight, and these arguments interfered with the Great Bear's well-deserved slumber.

The Great Bear sent a drought to the brown bears, which shrivelled the berries. She dried up the salmon streams. There was less food for all of the bears, so they had to learn to share, as the people had, in order to survive. But the bullying bears did not share. Because they were only cubs, they were selfish and immature. The starving brown bears grew thin and some of them died. There was wailing and moaning. It was impossible for the Great Bear to get any peace or rest.

The Great Bear reached down with her mouth, as mammals do with their young, and one by one she took the big, bullying bears in her jaws by the scruff of their necks. She shook each of the oversized bears vigorously to punish them and teach them a lesson. The big, bullying bears didn't look the same after they had been disciplined. They were still much bigger than the other bears, but now they also had large tufts of hair on their backs where the Great Bear had held them in her jaws. They were also slightly dishevelled.

The Great Bear separated all of these bigger bears and called them Grizzly Bears. The Grizzly Bears were now in direct competition with the brown bears for food. The cubs of the brown bears would never again have so much to eat that they became overgrown bullies. The constellation known as Hercules represents the huge, fierce, ruff-necked Grizzly Bear.

Tlingit

*E*arly today, I caught two small fish in the shallows. *I ate the two fish quickly. My stomach hurts more, not less, after the eating. Again the sky is blue. Again the sun makes the smooth shore rocks hot on the pads of my paws. Then I walk slowly toward the place of many bears. Soon it will be time to find the male white bear again. My body says yes, yes, again try the baby again, yes, though the not-thinking of K'ytuk is still strong.*

Now I am sensing and smelling for something to eat. Tlingit knows about the Mountain of Man Things, but I do not go there like the other white bears. There are man sounds there. There are men around. Beware of the danger. I need something to eat. Here the things to eat are strange—mostly non-fish things that taste of man. Never has Tlingit come to the Mountain of Man Things, but now it must be. The Way of Not Thinking becomes easier. Ignore the danger-dangers.

Think of nothing—think nothing. Walk slowly up Man-Thing Mountain. It is sharp on my paws. It is now slippery and now wet. Every step is different. I close my mouth and jaws on foodstuff. I chew and swallow strangeness. I chew, swallow, and survive. I chew, swallow, and survive.

I hear a loud crack of death. I am running away—running and running away. Running and running away!

Anne & Gilbert

Gilbert rolled over on his side and ate the cheese sandwich that Anne had brought him. He drank the soda, rolled onto his back, and then continued to contemplate the ceiling. He appeared to accept the sudden miraculous appearance of an attractive, plump blonde nursemaid.

She tried to engage him in conversation, cringing as she awkwardly fumbled around and then blushing at the silences that followed.

"Nice place you have here. I really like how you've fixed it up."

"Are these pictures of your kids? They seem like good kids."

It didn't take her long to grow tired of these polite niceties. "I guess you're pretty upset about the pipeline rupture. I am too. I left my job and my academic career behind to come here because of it. I don't even know what I can do."

He didn't ignore her. When she spoke, he looked directly into her inquisitive blue eyes, but his black eyes were flat and dead. It was disconcerting as hell. She had been struck by his distinguished-yet-rugged and confident masculinity from thousands of kilometers away. In person, he was nothing short of breathtaking. His face was full and he had handsome features. His long, tan muscular body was the thrilling antithesis of Anne's pale pink curvy softness. Although she had been shy at first, his complete lack of response soon dissolved her inhibitions, and she sat at his bedside and considered him with frank admiration. His shirt, fastened only by one button at the waist, revealed a smooth, hairless chest and one dark, taut nipple. Such risqué intimacy with a stranger entertained Anne for some time. After a while, confident that he wasn't suffering, and certain that he wouldn't be going anywhere, she stood up and stretched.

Tentative explorations of Gilbert's cabin soon turned into full-fledged snooping. By midafternoon, Anne had taken a full inventory of the fridge and the larder. She had familiarized herself with the contents of the various kitchen drawers and cabinets. An hour later, a self-guided tour of the yard and garden yielded a harvest of hardy Swiss chard leaves and a few lumpy, misshapen carrots. In the coolness of the evening, as the rice and carrots boiled and the salmon poached in a well-seasoned cast-iron pan, Anne discovered a wooden box full of photographs on a bookshelf, and she immersed herself in examining them. She flattened the curled edges and creating an imagined chronology out of the haphazard pile.

She found school pictures—headshots on a blue background—of two handsome children: a girl and a boy. She found fishing pictures of Gilbert and his son holding their catch on a sunny riverbank, grinning madly in one shot yet sober and serious in another. She found a picture of Gilbert waving from a half-constructed roof with snow-capped mountains in the background. She picked up a faded picture of Gilbert and an arrestingly lovely First Nations woman. She was shorter than he was, and she had smooth black hair. Half of it was piled on her head, and half of it was cascading down her trim back. They both were wearing blankets with intricate designs: black stylized animals on crimson backgrounds. She was holding a carved wooden object in one hand, and he was holding a carved wooden staff. They were standing before a great cedar tree with shaggy bark and green fronds. In another photo, they were seated on the front porch of the cabin with their arms around each other. They were laughing. She found a series of group shots around the base of a totem pole; she wondered if it was his extended family. Anne squinted and took her time picking out Gilbert and his beautiful partner in this photo. They were the youngest people in this picture. Most of the people in the picture were elderly women wearing ornate blankets.

She found another shot of the woman who must have been Gilbert's wife. She was leaning against a white pickup truck and not smiling. The glorious ebony curtain of hair was gone, and in its place was a blue bandana tied around her evidently naked scalp. Her chin was high and her expression was defiant. She was much thinner than she had been in the previous shots. Her cheeks were pale and hollow under her high, smooth cheekbones. She seemed to be daring the photographer to take the picture.

Anne was holding this photo and considering it when she sensed a presence behind her. She looked over her shoulder and said,

"Oh! You're up!" She scrambled to turn around in her chair.

Gilbert looked not at Anne but at the photograph she was holding. He then looked toward the tentative arrangement of pictures on his kitchen table.

Anne blushed. "I'm sorry, I just made myself at home. I didn't know when you would be getting up, and I was curious, so I just..." she trailed off.

He turned around and walked to the stove. He then turned off the heat under the salmon, removed two plates from a cupboard, and served the food. Anne hurried to return the photos to their box and set the table, her face hot with embarrassment. Gilbert poured two glasses of water and then they sat together and ate in silence. Toward the end of the meal, the awkwardness grew too intense for Anne.

"Listen," she said. "I don't have to stay here. I don't know why Little Ted brought me here. I'm sure I could find a hotel room. I'll just call a cab and be going." Her voice sounded small. To her it sounded thin, squeaky, and petulant.

Gilbert waited until she looked up from between her rounded shoulders. "No," he said. "Stay." Then he smiled quickly like the brief flash of a little fish jumping out of a flat lake. He left the table and went back into his bedroom, closing the door softly.

The ripples left behind by that smile kept Anne awake past midnight.

Churchill Northern Studies Centre, Churchill, Manitoba

It had been seven days since the spill and four days since Anne's departure. Ian nursed his third cup of coffee and surveyed the landscape before him, scanning for white specks in motion. Behind him, he heard the busy tapping of Jane's fingers on a keyboard.

The landscape in question was in flux—the green vegetation, the choppy water, the grey rocks, and the hot blue sky. I'm not as emotionally involved with this project as Anne, thought Ian, but I'm not detached as Jane. Anne herself is practically a polar bear sow, Ian thought to himself, grinning. Anne would hate to hear the word *sow* applied to her, conscious as she was of her ample curves. If she were here, Anne would have stood beside him at the window this morning and bemoaned the soaring mercury in the thermometer. She would have fretted openly about the ever-receding ice and the scarcity of habitat, and then she would have collected the data necessary to convince the world that greenhouse gases must be reduced in order to save these sleek, pure, beautiful bears. Instead, she was thousands of kilometers away, where she was probably up to her armpits in liquid black poison. It was a different facet, Anne had pointed out, of the same problem: the dependence on fossil fuels. Yet how had Anne reached Kitimat but through a series of carbon-burning aeroplane flights? As they said, if you were not part of the solution, you were part of the problem. This aphorism had been bouncing around between Ian's ears since Anne's departure.

Okay, okay, thought Ian. I use power sparingly at my house. I turn off lights, computers, and electrical appliances when I'm not using them. I take public transportation. Instead of driving, I ride my sleek black bicycle whenever and wherever I can. I try to buy local foods instead of the oranges that are flown into my kitchen from South Africa. And I'm not alone. There are lots of people like me who want to stop being dependent on power that wrecks this planet. There are not enough of us, though. There are nowhere near enough of us. Something as big and bad as this oil spill in Kitimat should inspire the public to change, shouldn't it? But polar bears will soon become extinct if we don't clean up our act. Shouldn't this announcement have the same impact as the oil spill?

Anne's departure left an enormous vacuum. It left a sad silence. The three of them had been in each other's company almost exclusively for weeks. He and Anne had developed a solid friendship. Her absence wasn't the only source of uneasy feelings creeping like snakes underneath Ian's skin. Jane was a nucleus of tight, compressed energy. She was like a star that was about to go supernova. Logically, Anne's leaving should have eased workplace tensions for Jane. The women had opposite approaches to just about everything, and they argued on an almost daily basis. Instead, Jane seemed to be seething. Ian looked over at her as she worked on her laptop. Her brow was furrowed, and her mouth was pulled sideways into a straight, determined line. Were those beads of sweat, Ian wondered.

Jane looked like she was being subtly tortured with bamboo strips driven underneath her toenails by invisible hands beneath the table. Ian couldn't stand it. "What's the matter, Jane?"

"Nothing." She kept typing and didn't look up. "I'm working, as you can see."

This kind of bristling used to drive Anne crazy. It didn't faze Ian at all. "Yes, I see that you are working. The expression on your face leads me to believe that something is amiss."

"Of course not. I am just concentrating." Jane paused, glanced up at Ian. The furrows on her forehead became deeper. "If you'll excuse me," she said, "I want to get this report finished today." She then went back to her computer screen. Ian was dismissed. Around herself, Jane erected an invisible force field that seemed to say, "Go away and don't pry." Ian considered the neat part of her short shiny black haircut: a thin white line of scalp. He was close enough to reach out and touch the sleeve of her purple fleece jacket. If he had had the audacity to reach out, Ian knew, there would be a blinding flash of blue-white light, and he would be thrown back violently against the wall. He would have to wait until she powered down her strong defenses.

Ian didn't feel like spending another day hiking over dwindling bear habitat. Like Anne, Ian sometimes felt frustrated about his inability to do something concrete that would immediately help the polar bears in their plight. As part of their commitment to the Northern Studies Centre, the scientists performed volunteer work for Churchill's Polar Bear Alert, a program that helped keep the community of Churchill safe from the threat of polar bear attacks. They chiefly did so by scaring interested bears away from the municipality and back into the wild. Ian donned an orange parka, a black wool skullcap, and black leather mittens. He then headed to the best place for polar bear viewing anywhere in the world: the former site of the Churchill municipal garbage dump.

The Churchill Dump was the ignominious location of the best polar bear viewing on the planet. The dump became popular with the bears, and shortly thereafter, the dump became popular with tourists and thrill seekers. Much had been done in the last decade to change this dangerous and vaguely embarrassing state of affairs. Proper tours for viewing polar bears were established, gawkers were discouraged, bears were scared away from the dump, and the dump itself was converted into a recycling and waste management facility. The bears still came, though. They were attracted by the inevitable food smells near the waste management building.

Firing a gunshot into the air usually had the desired effect of sending the bears loping off toward the shores of Hudson Bay, where slushy ice was already beginning to form.

Ideally, Ian knew, the bears would stay away from Churchill altogether. Before white people had come and settled permanently in this area, polar bears at this time of year would have been resting in day beds—wallows they create in willow thickets or kelp beds along the shores of the bay—rising occasionally to test the stability of the ice. When the polar bears shoved the ice with their massive, muscular forelegs, they learned what they needed to know about the thickness and stability of the ice. They would wait and watch. They would test the ice until it was time to venture out and hunt for seals. This ice-gauging behaviour always thrilled Ian when he observed it. It was so intelligent. It was so human.

Ian stopped at the Polar Bear Alert Office, signed out a rifle, and chatted with Frank Hobbes. Frank was a polar bear aficionado. He was an amateur enthusiast who worked tirelessly to keep Churchill and polar bears on friendly terms. He was an excellent resource for the Northern Studies Centre staff because he was able to recognize individual bears even from a good distance.

"We got a new female coming around," said Frank. "Really skinny and really skittish. Wouldn't get too close if I were you. She looks like she'd fight just as easily as flight. I'm thinking she needs a permanent move up to Wager Bay before she gets to be a problem. Better take a tranq dart gun with you just in case."

The air was crisp. The temperature was not quite cold enough to freeze the garbage solidly and thus suppress the smell. Ian wrinkled his nose as he approached the waste management building from his vehicle on foot. Visibility was excellent and it certainly was autumn. By Ian's initial count, there were four hungry bears and three giddy tourists. Ian's volunteer duties were twofold. First, his job was to approach the tourists, educate them about the dangers of viewing polar bears in this open setting, and provide them with information about alternative ways to view the animals in more natural settings in the Churchill area. He would conclude these sessions with a polite-yet-firm request that the tourists leave. He would warn them that he was about to fire his gun in order to chase the bears away from the area, and it was for the animals' own good. Most people were rational and respectful of the ferocity of the bears. Most people were also concerned for their own personal safety. Most people retreated immediately and thanked Ian for his troubles.

This morning Ian, however, wasn't quite so fortunate. On closer inspection, the European tourists consisted of three men around the ages of sixty or sixty-five years old. The tourists—Germans, Ian thought, guessing by the accents, had travelled a long way to see the polar bears, and they weren't easily persuaded to leave.

"Zey are not eenterested een us," one of the tourists said, shrugging.

"Not yet they aren't," Ian replied. "If they *do* get interested, however, they won't be coming over to shake your hand."

"We take ze photographs, zen we go," the tourist replied, lifting a large professional camera, pointing it at the bears, and zooming in.

"Listen," said Ian, glancing nervously at the group of polar bears. All of the bears had stopped milling around the big garage doors of the waste management building. They were standing stock-still and staring at the humans. "Those bears can run forty kilometers per hour when they charge. If they decide to be here, they'll be here in thirty seconds." Among the bears was a smallish bear; it was the skinny one that Frank had mentioned. Ian squinted. Unless Ian was mistaken, the new-to-civilization bear was none other than Tlingit. He wasn't as good at identifying individuals as Anne or Jane were, but he had seen enough photographs of the bear that Anne had become enamoured with. She had a little lopsided look to her muzzle, a smudge of greyish skin near her nose that was probably a scar from a fight. It was Tlingit all right, and Ian thought he could sense her tension.

"Gentlemen, I'm going to have to insist that you return to your vehicle at this point. I'm going to fire this gun overhead and I can't predict which way those bears will run." Ian took the safety off of the rifle loudly and obviously.

Another one of the men put his hand into the front pocket of his puffy, blue down parka, pulled out a half-eaten granola bar, peeled the foil wrapper back another inch or two, and took a leisurely bite. He then stared inanely at the white carnivores that were only the length of a parking lot away from him.

"What the hell? What are you—" Ian stopped short. It was too late. Tlingit had caught the scent of something edible, and she had caught the sense of something threatening. She charged.

Ian reacted immediately by firing two gunshots into the air. The other three bears turned away from town and ran toward the water. The charging bear stopped in her tracks. Fortunately, Ian didn't have to put a bullet in her to save his life and those of the tourists. He removed the tranquilizer gun from his shoulder, took aim, and then fired it into the bear's shoulder. The bear registered the pain and then continued her charge toward them.

Ian grabbed his canister of bear spray from his holster and braced himself. He heard the tourists screaming as they ran away behind him. Ian felt strangely calm. When they had first begun their residencies at the Northern Studies Centre, all of the scientists had received training for how to handle bear attacks. He knew that statistically his best chance of survival was a well-aimed blast of bear spray, and he knew that his tranq dart was already embedded in the bear's flesh.

He never had to spray her, though. The anaesthetic in the dart worked quickly. Confused, she slowed down, turned her head, and bit at the dart on her shoulder. He remained still and kept the spray canister ready. She was about thirty meters away, chewing at her shoulder. A long minute went by and then another minute passed. She began to roll her head from side to side. Relief washed through Ian's body as the bear collapsed. He radioed Frank.

"Bear down," he said. "South side of the waste building. I need restraining straps and tranq antidote. Do you copy?" His voice sounded more high-pitched than usual it usually did, but he was not screaming. It was nothing like the hysterical shrieking of the European tourists, whose loud voices had now been silenced. They were watching the scene unfold from the perceived safety of the interior of their rented pickup truck.

Beep bleep. Scratchy, low-key, and professional, Frank's voice came back over the radio. "Roger, Ian. Ten-four.

Proceeding to your location immediately. Our ETA is seven minutes."

Oh boy, thought Ian. Anne's not going to like this.

Gilbert and The Great Bear

The peaks and valleys of the lines and smudges on the ceiling of his bedroom lead Gilbert into the Land of Deep Sleep.

He is walking in the darkness and his senses are tingling. There are tiny pinpoints of light all around. They are even underfoot. He is walking in the stars and he is glittering, his movement scattering unbroken beams of light emitted from he knows not where. He feels the weightlessness of zero gravity. He takes slow steps and deep breaths. The soles of his feet are tingling. It is a pleasant coolness. The coolness is everywhere. The still air touches his skin everywhere. I am naked, Gilbert thinks. He is naked.

Far away in the distance, a star is swaying and moving toward him. It is walking with the same slow, steady steps that he is walking with. The star's gait is identical to his gait. It is as though he is moving closer to a mirror. Eventually, the star gets close enough for Gilbert to see that it isn't merely a star. The star is being held in the palm of a human hand. The human who is holding it is female. She is naked. Her full, dark breasts sway back and forth with the rhythm of her paces. The glow of the star illuminates her. There is a subtle shine to her long black tresses, and shadows are playing underneath the smooth curve of her belly. There is a glint of intelligence in her calm, dark eyes. It is the profile of a beautiful and familiar face. The star-holder is Clara.

Gilbert halts. He stretches out his arms and opens them. He thinks that his Clara will run into his embrace and place her smooth, warm cheek against his cool, flat chest. He thinks she will remain there peacefully and indefinitely, just like she used to, but instead she shakes her head. Then, from out of nowhere, a massive bear lumbers to her side, and she places her free hand on the bear's side, underneath the beast's shaggy, towering left shoulder.

Gilbert wants to go to Clara, but when he looks at the bear, its eyes catch his eyes, and he cannot tear his gaze away. The bear's coat is shimmering and changing from yellow to black to white to cinnamon. It is not any bear Gilbert recognizes. At the same time, it is every bear he has ever seen or heard of or read about. She—the Great Bear—is communicating with him somehow. He knows this bear is female, and he knows he cannot touch the bear the way that Clara is now touching it. He cannot get closer to his Clara, his love. Oh why not, he thinks. I miss her so. It is impossible for him to hold a star as Clara does.

Clara sways, holding the star in his peripheral vision, but the Great Bear is holding him somehow so that he cannot look away from her. Then she changes and becomes

Moksgm'ol, the spirit bear, and Gilbert gasps. This incarnation of Moksgm'ol is desperate, sad, and terrified all at once. Suddenly, Gilbert is made to understand his own infinitesimal sorrow compared to that of this beleaguered creature. The spirit bear raises one giant paw. The creamy fur is marred with a tarry substance. Then Clara begins to weep while stroking the bear's fur.

"Help him," Clara thinks. Gilbert hears her thoughts. "Help him!"

Moksgm'ol

I run beyond the range of mere men. Moksgm'ol can climb and reach where men cannot. Instinct and rage bring me here to a dark cool place that is closer to snow than water. There are many cedars and Sitka spruce. There are cool rocks and wet moss. I know this grove. It is farther from the riverbanks than I usually roam. As a cub the mother of Moksgm'ol took us to many different eating and sleeping places. She taught us well where we might hide.

I stop running and the disgusting odour of men is still with me. It is emanating from my own paws. There is something on my paws that has rendered them dark at the edges, and now that I have stopped I feel a stinging on the pads of my paws. I feel a stinging and I want to assuage it by licking it. I feel that I should not do this, yet the stinging must be assuaged. I touch *my tongue to the blackness on my left forepaw. My mouth is burning! It is the taste of death! Moksgm'ol is too far from rivers to drink cool water! I lick the leaves of the shrubs. I lick the bark of trees. My throat is burning and my paws stink. What manner of man's madness is this?*

As if from the past, when I was a soft stumbling cub, I hear my own whimpering. I hear the squeaking cries of a creature besieged. For shame! For shame! I run again. I stop in a clearing and shake my head from side to side, trying—oh trying—to escape the infernal fumes that are attached to this blackness that is attached to me, Moksgm'ol! Will I climb as far as the snowline to find relief? I will! I will reach the snow, though now it is the Time of the Valley Bottom. Moksgm'ol will reach the coldness and the purity of the high places of rock and snow.

Anne & Gilbert

Woken by birdsong and startled by her surroundings, when Anne opened her eyes it was just after dawn. She prepared coffee, and ate crisp sliced fall apples and toast. Her blonde hair hung loosely and softly around her rosy cheeks. She stood barefoot on the broad wooden planks in jean shorts and a white shirt. Stripes of golden autumn sunlight were slanting into the kitchen. She was attempting to think creatively about how to snap her handsome host out of his catatonic state. The ideas she was coming up with were unorthodox and inappropriate. Unconventional approaches rarely slowed her progress. It was the fear that her methods would backfire somehow that kept her from opening that bedroom door and carrying out an experiment or two.

Just then the bedroom door opened and he emerged.

"I had a dream last night about a bear," said Gilbert as a morning salutation. It felt conversational and familiar, as though he had known her for years. It was as though he hadn't been stretched out and unresponsive for hours the day previous.

The little woodstove had kept the cabin comfortably warm overnight. Gilbert wore a pair of cut-off shorts and nothing else. Anne kept the man's muscular bare legs and smooth, tan chest firmly in her peripheral vision. She looked instead directly into his chiselled face. It was all cheekbones and smooth dark skin.

"Really?" she asked, feigning nonchalance. "What happened?"

"Well, I think it was two bears, actually." Gilbert helped himself to a handful of apple slices. "It was a bigger one that was with my late wife Clara. You were looking at her pictures last night." Anne blushed. "And another one—a spirit bear—that had oil on its paws. I think the big one was the Great Bear."

"The Great Bear?"

"The spiritual mother of us all. There's a whole mythology that you might not be familiar with. What did you say your name was?" Gilbert asked with mild curiosity.

"Oh my goodness. Anne McCraig. I am so sorry I never even introduced myself. Anne. You can call me Anne. And you're Gilbert. I'm afraid I had the advantage." Anne extended a formal hand toward her host. He took it unconventionally between both of his hands; one hand pressed her palm, while the other hand covered the top of her hand warmly and gently. It was a gesture so intimate and tender that Anne almost pulled away out of modesty. Instead, she allowed herself to feel the energy between herself and Gilbert Crow. There was a lot of energy between them, thought Anne. Nerve endings were tingling. Synapses were firing. Chemical changes of various types were occurring simultaneously. He looked directly into her eyes and released her hand.

"We must go help the spirit bear with the oily paws today," said Gilbert.

"But that was just a dream!" Anne protested.

Gilbert fixed Anne with an earnest stare. "Dreams are as real as you and I. This morning is a dream that we are both dreaming. Last night I dreamed about the spirit bear with oil on its paws. The bear was dreaming that dream too. The bear and I were in the same dream because I must help it. You are here because you are part of the same dream."

"I see," said Anne. The scientific and skeptical part of her mind thought it was nonsense. "How will we find this bear, and how will we help it when we do?" She busied herself by buttering the toast. He would read her disbelief if he could see her eyes.

"The Great Bear and Clara will lead us to this troubled bear," Gilbert answered as he took the toast that she had just buttered. He waited for her to make eye contact. "You don't look convinced."

"One, I hardly know you. Two, according to Little Ted, you're supposed to be in a grief-induced catatonic state." Poor bereaved man, thought Anne. It's his grief that's making him think he can magically find the bear that was in a dream with his dead wife.

"One," said Gilbert, swallowing his toast hungrily, "you know me well enough to move into my house and go through my stuff while I'm sleeping. Two, you don't know Little Ted. He's the worst kind of matchmaking busybody you can imagine, regardless of his gender. Little Ted would hook your grandmother up with the Big Bad Wolf."

"So, we will find the spirit bear," Gilbert continued. "Then it will have to be tranquilized so that we can get the oil off of its paws. At that point we can relocate it. I'm thinking Princess Royal Island would be the best place for this bear. That way it won't be tempted to return to Kitimat and the oily water anytime soon. Thanks for making breakfast, by the way." Gilbert helped himself to more apple slices and another piece of toast.

"My pleasure," said Anne automatically. "And let's see. One, thank you for your impromptu, unwitting hospitality." Gilbert nodded, chewing slowly and deliberately. "Two, I'm glad you're not in some kind of emotional coma. I've a good mind to call up Little Ted and invite myself over to sleep on *his* couch."

"Don't do that," said Gilbert quickly. "You really are welcome here. Little Ted interferes, but he means well. I had the blues, and I did need someone or something to snap me out of them. You're here to help clean up the spill, correct?"

Anne told him about her academic background in biology, her internship at the Churchill Northern Studies Centre, and her compulsion to come and help when she heard about the spill. She omitted the emotionally charged subject of Tlingit.

"A bear specialist! Fantastic! The Great Bear truly did send you to help!" exclaimed Gilbert, delighted. His eyes sparkled with hope. It was misplaced optimism in Anne's opinion. But the man was growing more genuine—and more handsome—by the minute.

"The Great Bear," ventured Anne. "Is that a First Nations legend from around here?"

"Not exactly," Gilbert answered. "Clara's grandmother told us stories about the Great Bear. She was ninety-two years old when she began to tell us the stories. I was surprised because I had never heard them before. She died a few months later. She told us that her own grandmother took a spirit bear as a lover, and that bear told her grandmother the stories." He stretched. His powerful arms extended toward the ceiling. His eyes were closed. His silky black hair was so long that it brushed the denim waistband of his shorts.

This revelation further flustered Anne. "A woman and a bear?" she asked, as Gilbert came out of his stretch.

"It's probably a metaphor—a dream-story," Gilbert said, amused at Anne's disconcerted expression. He pursed his full lips into a smile and said, "It's probably not actual bestiality."

"Well, I suppose we should get going then," Anne said, aware of the pinking of her cheeks. "If we're going to find this bear today, I mean." If we stay I'll probably humiliate myself by attempting to kiss you, she thought to herself.

"Right." Gilbert disappeared into the bedroom and reappeared wearing work clothes. "I'll be waiting outside in my truck," he said, his tone sober and businesslike. Then he was out the door. Anne hastened to put on some practical clothing and then she joined him.

A quarter of an hour later, Anne had her first glimpse of the severity of the spill. The volunteer tent was abuzz with activity when she and Gilbert first entered it. Then someone—it must have been a local, thought Anne—recognized Gilbert. There was a hushing and a whispering. There was an awkward lowering of voices and averting of eyes; it was the social discomfort of the immediacy of a death. It was as if Gilbert had lost his beloved wife only a day or so previously. As they put on coveralls, boots, and breathing masks, the muttering continued in this atmosphere of mourning. Gilbert became engaged in a quiet conversation in a corner of the tent.

Anne wandered outside and peered into the forest. The lushness of the greenery and the stature of the trees made her feel—after her year perched on the flat, scrubby shores of Hudson Bay—like she had been transported to another planet. Cedar branches swooped down gracefully, elegant as forest dancers. There were sprays of fern in the undergrowth, which was a lush, thick carpet. Sitka spruce towered overhead. Their bottom needles were so far above Anne's head that she became dizzy looking up their metre-thick trunks.

Her practical eye quickly saw the tragedy behind the temperate rainforest. Thick articulated plastic hoses snaked through the undergrowth. One end of each of them was attached to a suction truck. The trucks were emitting industrial whines; a diesel pump was rumbling. At least fifty or sixty people wearing orange vests were toiling in the trees. Some people carried buckets stained at the rims with brown-black sludge. Even through the filters of her mask, the overwhelming fumes of fuel assaulted Anne's olfactory sense.

Suddenly and silently Gilbert was beside her. He spoke without preamble. "A spirit bear actually was seen running north the first day of the spill. My friend Gary can fly over the area where the bear might be tomorrow and try to locate it. In the meantime, let's see what we can do here to help." Anne smiled wryly. It's not just a dream, then, she thought.

The cleanup crew were using a path of wood chips to travel on foot between the river and the spill. About halfway to the river, they passed a couple of volunteers shovelling up oily wood chips and spreading fresh new ones. The masks made it nearly impossible to determine the mood of the volunteers because their faces were obscured. Anne intuited that the atmosphere was mostly grim. It was a sort of depressed resignation. *Or maybe I'm projecting.*

As they approached the river, the amount of sunlight filtering through the trees increased. Anne gasped. Suddenly, it was possible to see the enormity of the task. Everywhere one looked at the ground, pools of black liquid glinted and glimmered, revealing their characteristic macabre rainbows. She and Gilbert walked out onto the expanse of smooth, round rocks on the shore of the river. Dozens of people armed with hoses and buckets were lifting the rocks one by one and washing the oil off of them. The clean rocks were placed in clean buckets. Other volunteers with larger hoses were pressure-washing the shore and diverting the oil into hollows that yet more volunteers had created with shovels.

Out on the water, two lines of boats were visible. One line was heading upriver and the other was heading downriver. At first glance, Anne was relieved to see that booms were in place from the south bank to the north bank in both directions. The spill's infiltration of the previously clean and pristine Kitimat River seemed limited and contained. She and Gilbert obtained buckets and hoses and joined the rock-washers. They didn't speak. Anne snuck in a glance at Gilbert once in a while. His face remained flat and impassive.

Every so often, a shout would ring out from one of the boats. Around noon, Anne heard a strangled yell of horror mingled with disgust. She looked up and saw a man leaning over the gunwales of a small aluminum boat. He held a net out over the water; a fish was in it. The fish wasn't thrashing wildly like a freshly netted fish should. There might have been a slow-motion tail flick, but Anne wasn't close enough to see if there was any movement in its gills. The slow black viscous drips from the fish were visible, though, and the surface of the fish was unnaturally smooth and glossy. It was completely coated in oil. All of its scales were obscured. Anne had to turn her head. She felt tears prickling in her eyes. She was aware of Gilbert, who had stopped and was now standing and watching the oil-asphyxiated fish suspended over the river.

He had known the Kitimat River his whole life. These were the waters in which his mother had washed him. These were the waters in which his grandmother had rinsed the berries they had collected together. On this very shore he had stood with his grandfather, and from this water he had pulled his first fish. On these rocks, his father and grandfather had taught him how to clean the fish, and that very evening they had all eaten its delicate white meat. This water was where he had waded with his father and heard the stories of his ancestors. This was where, years later, he and Clara had taken Max and Charlotte and told them the same stories, and the children had laughed at the antics of all of the animals. They had pretended to fly, swim, and climb like the birds, fish and beasts.

A bald eagle flew overhead just then. Its scream was a piercing, mournful keen. It was as if, Gilbert thought, the bird were protesting the contamination of his food chain.

Gilbert followed the bird's flight until it came to rest heavily on the upper branch of a tree hanging over the river. The eagle turned his majestic white head slowly and imperiously, surveying this strange invasion of his fishing grounds. He issued another long cry from the sharp curves of his great yellow beak. It reminded Gilbert of another story, and he began, for Anne's sake, to tell it.

The Great Bear Gives Eagle his Cry

The bears of the earth were proud of their place in the circle of life on earth. Smaller creatures either bowed before the terrible majesty of the bears or they scuttled away in awe and fear. The bears began to think that they were superior to all of the other creatures of the earth. One particular creature's existence troubled them, though, and that Creature was Eagle.

The bears were jealous that Eagle could fly. When the salmon were scarce the bears saw Eagle fly out over the water, where he fished and caught wonderfully big and juicy salmon, which the Bears themselves could not have caught from the shore. Many times Eagle would swoop down make a kill or steal food right from under a bear's muzzle. After a while, the bears became so envious of Eagle that they began to complain.

The bears were not aware that Eagle was the Great Bear's messenger. The Great Bear had created Eagle to be strong and swift. She had given her creature an extraordinary flying ability so that she might quickly and efficiently be informed of developments on earth. It was Eagle who informed the Great Bear that the bears of the earth had become especially jealous of Eagle. The Great Bear was amused. Overcoming obstacles was part of life's journey, so she did nothing. She thought it would be good for the bears to overcome this obstacle of jealousy as part of their journey.

Eagle learned from the Great Bear that the bears of the earth would not be satisfied in their longing for wings to fly, and when Eagle related this news to the other eagles of the earth, the eagles decided to have some fun with the bears. The silent, soaring birds began to swoop down to quietly and intentionally startle the bears. Spotting a bear stalking a fish in the river, an eagle would time its deadly dive perfectly so that it could steal its fish. When executed with perfect timing, this stealing of meals would fluster and enrage the bear. Still not content, the eagle would fly to a nearby branch and eat the fish in full view of the bear that it had stolen the fish from. The bears were livid. They roared deafeningly and angrily toward the sky. The Great Bear heard them and she watched and thought about what to do.

The Great Bear had given Eagle the gift of a silent approach in order to make her creature more lethal. Now she called Eagle to her.

"You have the mightiest wings, the most savage beak and claws, and the clearest and sharpest vision of any of the creatures of the air. I am now going to give you a unique and loud cry, and I am going to compel you to use it so that all of the creatures on the surface of the earth will know that Eagle is near. It will make your journey on the earth more challenging and therefore more interesting."

Eagle's beak opened and a loud, high-pitched call issued forth. The bears of the earth looked up and knew that Eagle was nearby. Then the bears laughed and were content again with their place on the earth.

"Thank you," said Anne, her voice muffled by her breathing mask. "That was a very good story." She looked directly into his eyes. He looked directly into her eyes. Her skin tingled and her stomach dropped. This man—this human being—was making a connection with her. There was curiosity. There was interest tinged with excitement. There was a hot spark and plenty of dry tinder.

Moksgm'ol

The infernal slick blackness cannot be purged from the paws of the mighty Moksgm'ol! My polluted paws fouled the cold white snow, yet the blackness and the reek remain. Again and again I have passed my muzzle against the poison and attempted to remove it. My eyes smart *and weep, and my nose burns. I am angry and I roar with displeasure.*

O Man, your noises despoil the rustle and hum of the forest. The lapping and gurgling of the waters are drowned by your ugly sounds. O Man, your hard grey roads bring flashes of speeding light and sudden death to all manner of creatures.

O Man! O Man, your machines rip down the trees that are my home, and the forest which has for all time been Moksgm'ol's sanctuary and birthright. O Man, you tear away the berry bushes. You destroy the soft fruits of the undergrowth and leave us wandering around hungry.

O Man, what manner of madness is this evil toxin that violates the purity of my paws, spread out in sinister silence along the very ground where we must walk?

I retreat to my place that is the safest and the farthest removed from all other creatures. My energy has been stolen and my strength has been sapped by this violation of Moksgm'ol. I cannot even sleep in my accustomed defensive ball. I must extend my forepaws to distance them from my beleaguered face.

Jonathan Fuhrenmann

"I'm lucky, I know. I know, man! I know how lucky I am." Jonathan's voice was scratchy and impatient. The smile faded from the glossy pink lips of the pretty young nurse who had come to check the bandages on his thigh.

"Doesn't *seem* like it," she said, hurt by her patient's ungrateful tone. She pressed the dressing down firmly, briefly checked his vital signs, and disappeared through the opening in the green curtains. Jonathan wanted to call her back and explain to her precisely how often he was told about his unbelievably good fortune. The laughing emergency room doctor had said, "I thought I had seen it all! You're the luckiest son of a bitch I've ever met!" The obnoxious reporter and photographer from the local news rag had said, "So you just decided to pitch your tent in some random place in the forest—in grizzly bear country. Is that correct?" Then, in a confidential whisper, lowering his little digital recording device, he had said, "You must have golden horseshoes up your ass, buddy." His own *mother,* for Christ's sake, had said over the telephone, "Punctures, scratches, and bruises? That's all? My God, Jonathan, you lead a charmed life. You gave me a heart attack, do you realize that?"

He lifted up the bandages that the nurse had just replaced. There were four long lacerations and several black stitches in each of them. The thigh was puffy, yellow, and green between each long claw mark. It was not infected, though, the doctor had said. He was bruised and traumatized. His left ankle was taped up. He couldn't see the twenty-eight puncture wounds and the purple bruising, but he could feel it throbbing.

"Too bad Old Griz got you on different legs," the doctor said. "Walking's going to be slow and a little painful for two or three weeks. Still." The doctor chortled and shook his head. "You're so damn lucky! You know what he would have done next? He would have scalped you. Yep, once a grizzly's got you in the clear, they go for the head and neck. It would have been game over then, Jonathan my boy. Or at least you would have been mutilated and disfigured," he mused.

The Kitimat Health Centre emergency room was much busier than usual, Jonathan learned through eavesdropping. The beds around him were full of people suffering from poisoning through the inhalation of toxic fumes from the oil spill. The cleanup crew were supposed to wear breathing protection, but not all of them were doing this consistently and not everyone was affected equally.

After three days in the Health Centre, Jonathan was released. He announced his intention to join the oil spill cleanup crew immediately, and the doctor shook his head. "I don't think so, Jonathan. You can't risk wading in the river and infecting these wounds. You won't be able to spend all day standing or walking. You should go home and heal up, my boy. Seems like there's plenty of people volunteering to help out."

"No, man, I'm staying. There's got to be something I can do."

A nurse—not the young pretty one but an older, sensible-looking woman with short grey hair—stood beside the doctor. "Sure. Where are you going to stay?"

Jonathan's brain was still fuzzy from painkillers and addled from the bear attack. He hadn't even thought about his tent, which likely lay in ribbons right where he had staked it. Thinking about the remains of his tent brought back the memory of the bear's claws ripping through the blue nylon. He remembered the appearance of its enormous muzzle. The colour drained from his face and he sank back onto the bed.

"Take care of yourself, Jonathan," said the nurse, placing a folded pair of pale blue hospital scrubs on his legs. "You can keep those or return them if you don't want them. The track pants you were wearing were destroyed. Do you want me to call you a cab?"

The Volvo was still parked on the road close to where he had been attacked. The keys were stashed under the back bumper, but the thought of returning to the scene of the attack made his stomach clench with fear.

"Uh, sure," said Jonathan. "Uh, has anyone seen—I mean, do you guys know, where the, uh, bear is?"

The doctor smiled wryly. "We've got a situation on our hands here in Kitimat, as you know. I would guess there's no one on hand to track your grizzly. It was nice to meet you, Jonathan. I'd wish you good luck but you already have loads of the stuff!" He shook Jonathan's hand, and then he turned and strode away.

"The cab's on the way," said the nurse, smiling affectionately at the doctor's wit.

Slowly and gently, Jonathan eased the soft blue pyjama pants over his tender legs and hobbled toward the exit. Brilliant fall sunshine was pouring in through the tall glass doors, which slid open at his approach. Outside, Jonathan blinked and peered in both directions for his taxi. Directly in front of the exit stood a mountain of a man with a gloss of sweat on his corpulent face. He pushed a pair of dark-rimmed prescription glasses up his nose, unfolded a broad arm, and waved a hand as big as a pork roast. He almost obscured the beat-up burgundy four-door sedan he was leaning on.

"Hey. You the guy who needs a cab?"

* * *

Beads of perspiration began forming on Jonathan's forehead and the sweat poured freely in his armpits as Little Ted pulled his taxicab up beside Jonathan's abandoned car. Trees loomed over the road. There was darkness under the canopy and trickery in the shadow and light that created hiding places for any manner of beast. Jonathan's aches and pains began to flare up. He wondered if he had been too impulsive in leaving the hospital, but he decided that he couldn't have spent another day getting mocked and harassed by the rotating medical staff. This hulking cab driver showed sincere interest and concern, which was refreshing. There was no snickering and no bear-attack advice offered in glaring hindsight. There were no admonishments, but there was also no sympathy.

"So, I guess you're going to need a motel room now?" Little Ted asked. "You didn't bring a spare tent with you, eh?"

Jonathan's options were few, and he quickly shuffled through them now in his mind. He could drive back down to

Vancouver and retreat ignominiously with his tail between his legs like a frightened and defeated squirrel, but this was his least favourite option. He had to be able to lend a hand with the oil spill cleanup in some capacity, even if it were from behind a desk or in a kitchen making sandwiches. Remaining in Kitimat in a costly rented room, however, was financially impractical and—honestly—impossible. *Purchasing another tent and attempting once again to camp isn't going to be something I can do either, though. I am too chicken to get out of this guy's cab right now and walk two meters to the Volvo. That bear might be drooling just out of sight behind that clump of ferns over there.*

Little Ted put his vehicle in park and turned it off. The windows were rolled down. Birds rustled in the undergrowth, calling to each other in happy chirps. A soft whisper of wind rustled through high branches. Seconds and then minutes ticked by. Jonathan stared out of the passenger seat window at the unbridgeable gulf between the two vehicles. A heap of fabric was wedged between the back bumper and the ground. Jonathan tried not to look at what must be the remains of his tent and bedding, which had been thoughtfully stashed by the forestry workers who had scared his ursine attacker away. Little Ted was silent and patient. Glints of mischief were hidden well behind the thick lenses of his glasses.

"I guess no one has seen that bear," remarked Little Ted.

"No," Jonathan said in one glum little syllable.

"It could still be around then."

"Mm-hmm."

"You got your keys on you?" asked Little Ted.

"Uh, no," said Jonathan. "They're hidden on top of the rear passenger tire."

"I'll go see if they're still there," offered Little Ted after a longish silence. Jonathan opened his mouth to object, but then he closed it. His injuries smarted as if the pain had grown worse because he was near the place where they had been inflicted. Little Ted lumbered out of his cab, leaving the driver's side door open. A tinny pinging alarm sounded because the door was ajar. The alarm comforted Jonathan; he imagined it was a human sound that was strange enough to scare away any interested fauna, such as a giant grizzly bear with a taste for pale white flesh. Jonathan didn't turn his head to watch Little Ted's progress. Tense and immobile, he sat there listening to the heavy steps, the fumbling around, the sound of car doors opening and closing, and then finally the ignition sound of his own car.

"She started up no problem at all!," announced Little Ted, as if there had been a question—as if Jonathan's difficulty with proceeding to his own car had been a mechanical problem. "Get in there, Jonathan. Then follow me."

"Thanks," said Jonathan. "Uh, where are we going?"

"I think I know a place where you can crash for a couple of days until you feel up to helping mop up the mess," said Little Ted.

"Okay," said Jonathan. He lurched out of the cab and got behind the wheel of his car, quickly slamming the door shut.

As they drove back toward Kitimat's town centre, it occurred to Jonathan that he had never spoken a word to the cab driver about his determination to help with the cleanup.

They pulled up in front of a small, tidy A-frame log house. It was so small, Jonathan thought, it was practically a cabin. Little Ted walked up to the front door and opened it without knocking or giving a salutation of any kind. He looked around inside for a moment and then called back to Jonathan.

"Yep, you can stay here. This is my friend Gilbert's place. You tell him Little Ted brought you here. He's got someone else from out of town staying on his couch, but you still have your bedroll and pillow, yes?" Little Ted raised an interrogative eyebrow. His glasses immediately slid down his nose.

"Are you sure?" Jonathan asked. He was already extracting his damaged sleeping bag, his dirt-and-needle encrusted foam mattress, and his wrinkled pillow from the back of the Volvo.

"Yeah. Gilbert likes to help people out. You'll see. Cook up something for dinner if you feel up to it. There are plenty of groceries. Here's my card if you need a ride again for some reason." Little Ted handed Jonathan a business card. "See you."

Little Ted sat in his taxicab and fiddled with his cell phone for a few minutes, pretending not to watch the skinny young man with his stringy long hair as he limped between the cabin and his car and made himself at home.

The Great Bear Brings Wolf to the World

People were slow to learn how to live in the world after the Long Cold Time. They continued to use the other creatures of the earth toward their own ends. They were more grateful than they had been before for the hides of Bear and Beaver and Deer. They were grateful for the flesh of Fish, for the tall strong trees, and for the powerful feathers of Eagle. However, people were still sometimes wasteful of these great gifts of nature. People were fearful of the other creatures of the earth, and they felt separate from them. The Great Bear saw the people's fear, and so she thought about creating a friend for them.

The Great Bear observed how people had chosen to live in families, which gathered together as clans. She created Wolf, a social animal that lived in packs, respected their leaders, and organized themselves the same way that people did. The Great Bear gave Wolf the instinct to scavenge, and she instilled in Wolf a certain sense of boldness.

Smelling food and curious about the inhabitants, Wolf came to the outskirts of the human villages. Wolf fed on bones and hides discarded by people. Human children noticed Wolf, and they were delighted with this new creature. While the adults of the villages spent busy days hunting, fishing, cooking, and sewing, the children enticed Wolf closer and closer to the villages.

One day when the adult wolves were hunting, their puppies came to play with the human children on the outskirts of the village. The wolf puppies drew closer and closer to the children, eventually allowing the children to touch them and pick them up. The human children were delighted, and they brought the soft, grey puppies into the village to show their parents.

The adult people were amazed that their children could handle wild creatures, and they were won over by the innocent youth of the puppies. They allowed the children to keep the wolf puppies in their arms.

The adult wolves then returned to their den to find their puppies missing. They followed their puppies' scent to the village, where the people were gathered around a fire, telling stories and singing songs. The wolves' fear of fire was outweighed by parental instinct, and they circled the people, baring their sharp fangs. Their yellow eyes were glowing angrily.

The Chief of the village was wise. He told the children to return the puppies to their parents. The pacing, snarling wolves terrified the human children, and they released the puppies to their parents. The next day, however, the same thing happened. The puppies played with the children during the day, and the wolves came to retrieve their pups at night. Some pups returned to the villages to stay, and these wolves became dogs.

With its sharp snout and long, full, curving tail, the constellation Leo is known as The Wolf.

Yukuai

Something is different today, but it isn't the kind of difference that is good or interesting. It is different in a bad way. This morning it is agonizing to move. I wake on my side underneath the shelter, and the lumps of pain inside my skin have become fireballs. I somehow manage to stand on four paws and move to the fence place for feeding. When the noisy rolling man-thing comes with the bamboo, however, I find that I cannot move toward the crunchy greenness that he throws in, and I find that I do not care. The bamboo-throwing man doesn't notice my lethargy.

The crowds arrive. My vision is blurrier than it has ever been. The crowds of people bring their usual cacophony and fetid odours, but I am immobile. I am trying to be invisible. I am trying to disappear.

"Mommy what's wrong with the panda?"

A female voice responds. "Beats me, Charlie. He looks depressed. Brian! Brian! Come look at this panda!"

A man in a hat says in a bored drawl, "Ha! This sign says that bear's name is Yoo Koo Eye. It's Chinese for happy. Ha. That's the saddest bear I've ever seen!"

Another woman, a woman I have smelled before, ambles over to the growing knot of curious humans standing by my enclosure. "Happy," she croons. I recognize her voice. She has spoken to me on many occasions. I sense that she is kind. "Happy, how are you?"

"Hey, do you work here?" The man in the hat accusingly addresses the kind-voiced woman. "What the hell is wrong with your panda?"

The kind-voiced woman observes me for a few minutes. She doesn't reply to the rude man's question. I cannot move. I remain upright. The lumps of pain within me are searing live coals.

"This is bull crap. Come on, Wanda. It's just some panda! It doesn't even move! It looks like it's fake. Your panda looks fake!" The man hurls his final insult over his shoulder as he leads his family off toward the next enclosure.

Now my forelegs can no longer support my weight. They buckle underneath me. My head and chest hit the concrete. The impact and the momentum topple me entirely. The excruciating pain of fire licks at me from inside my body! A shrill voice is calling out somewhere outside of my enclosure.

Then there are humans. They are here inside my enclosure. I sense them. All of my instincts and experiences are screaming at me to attack and become free. I feel like harming them before they harm me, which is always what they do. My brain fires insistent signals, but my limbs only twitch in response.

"He's still moving, Stan. Get out the dart gun. We can't take any chances."

There is a sharp report and another tiny sting of pain, followed by blissful, merciful oblivion.

Anne, Gilbert & Jonathan

"Hi. I'm Jonathan. Uh, Little Ted said I could stay here, so I just put my stuff over there beside the bookshelf, okay? I made a salad and some grilled cheese sandwiches for dinner. Your garden is sweet."

Gilbert considered the lanky young white man who was addressing Anne as though this house belonged to her, a biologist from Ontario. Photographs of himself, Clara, Max, and Charlotte hung in prominent locations about the cabin.

"No points for observational skills, Jonathan. This is my place. My name's Gilbert Crow." He indicated Anne. "This is Anne. She's visiting from out east." Gilbert shook his head slowly as it dawned on him that Little Ted wasn't dropping wandering, confused misfits on his doorstep for the benefit of the wandering, confused misfits.

"Oh, sorry, man. Well, you've got a sweet place." Jonathan produced a strained attempt at a winning smile, a facial contortion that ended with a wince.

"Excuse me for asking," said Anne, "but are you hurt?"

The story of the grizzly bear attack unfolded over the evening meal. Jonathan's embarrassment was palpable as Anne and Gilbert listened gravely. Anne related several polar bear attack stories she had heard in Churchill. Gilbert asked for details and Anne provided them until Gilbert noticed an unhealthy greenish pallor stealing over Jonathan's complexion.

"You need to sleep, I think," said Gilbert. The young man nodded and hobbled to his makeshift bed on the floor. He stretched out and fell asleep within minutes.

Gilbert and Anne gravitated to the front porch. Outside, a red and purple twilight stretched out across the western sky. The mountains to the north and east were already shrouded in darkness. Their jutting silhouettes were an inkier black than the indigo sky background. Yellow-white pinpoint stars were beginning to tell their stories from millions of miles away.

Wearing sweaters and jeans and sitting in matching aromatic cedar chairs, they leaned back and talked. Their anecdotes and amusing stories led from one to the next like silver links in the endless chain that is possible between new friends. There was a thrill of unfamiliarity in the depths of fresh pairs of interested eyes. The bell of her laughter and the deeper resonance of his laughter mixed well. Many unlikely events had led up to these two people passing the invisible frontier beyond which a kiss becomes a possibility. Once lips meet, things begin to accelerate down the highway of desire.

It happened. Evening became night and then there was the lateness of the hour. Both of them were exhausted from physical labour and the mental fatigue of processing the oily nightmare on the river. They each were experiencing an emotional maelstrom. Their words emerged more slowly and they were punctuated by yawns. Anne confessed the need to sleep and Gilbert proffered an arm to help her stand. Palms touched, muscles flexed, and bodies moved closer in space. Hands remained clasped beyond mere politeness, and the free hands also met and held. There was an exploration, an exchange of breath, and an acknowledgement of the agreeable nature of each other's human perfume. A pink finger traced a cherry-chocolate lip. A nut-brown hand combed through a silky hank of honey-yellow hair. Lips met and arms pulled bodies closely together. Waves and currents began flowing.

Sweet hesitant kisses came in a crescendo of pressing passion. Gilbert pulled back and suggested that they go for a walk. Hand in hand for a quarter of an hour, they maintained some shy discussion about appropriateness, advisability; a decision was quickly and easily reached. They decided not to be cautious. They opened themselves to the possibility of becoming lovers. As they walked back toward the cabin through deserted midnight streets, their footsteps were a little quicker and her breath was a little shallow. His pulse was racing.

They tiptoed up the porch steps. Inside, they could hear gentle, childlike snores from the mattress in the corner. In the bedroom, where only yesterday Anne had looked down in admiration at a supine stranger, the length of both their bodies stretched out and the exploration began. There were forays beyond buttons. Fabric was tugged and pulled away from flesh. They were mutually amazed at the vast and wondrous differences in hue, shape, and firmness. He mapped the creamy, soft, curving lines of her body. In his muscles, bones, sinews, and blood flow, she charted the strength of his taut light-brown body. They mapped each other wordlessly and in awe of all creation. They created something new for themselves.

Dawn was pinking up the profile of the mountains when this first foray into their new world played itself out. Gilbert curled his longer body around the soft harbour of her back, one arm securely cupped around a breast.

A few hours later, they were woken by the clumsy sounds of utensils rattling and crockery breaking. Gilbert listened without reacting to the first two loud splintering sounds, but when he heard a third sound he sprang out of bed, slid on his jean shorts, and opened the bedroom door. Jonathan was right outside the door, poised to open it and apologize for reducing his host's kitchen inventory.

"Oh, hey man. Morning." Jonathan smiled brightly. "Hey, I broke, like, a cup and a plate. Sorry, man. My bum legs are kind of throwing me off." He shook his head and tossed the ropes of his uncombed hair away from his eyes so that he could peer over Gilbert's naked shoulder and get a better look at Anne's wide-eyed, blushing face. She was holding the twisted sheets at her neckline to cover the mounds of her breasts. The brief veil of confusion on the young man's face fell to reveal complete understanding.

"Hi!" Jonathan greeted Anne, waving and oblivious of her embarrassment. Then he said to Gilbert, "Cool. Uh, does this mean I can have the couch now?"

Tlingit

I need to eat again. Nothing. There is nothing. Today, not wanting to return to Man Mountain, I hear loud sounds. There were dangers yesterday but also things to eat. There are other bears also at Man Mountain finding food. *There are* bears waiting for ice. Slow ice never comes. Why is ice slow? Why am I waiting?

Again I go to Man Mountain today. There is nothing for eating outside the Man Place. Food smells mean food. With smells of nourishment, food must be here. Other bears are also here. They must know about the food and be eating.

I see man-shapes: one, two, three man-shapes. O danger. I am thinking only of danger and hunger. There is always nothing for eating, and here there is strangeness in the closeness of man-shapes. There is another one! Oh, go away. Go away. Now there is the aroma of something delicious. I am running toward the men. Boom! Boom! A loud loud noise! Oh, it's loud. So loud and—

I feel the pain of something terrible—*something* stinging and burning like the big bite of an insect.

Sleep comes now. Why sleep? It is so strange to sleep now. I wish I were not close to men—not descending into sleep now, near men. Please don't go to sleep now.

Ah.

Churchill Northern Studies Centre

"You didn't have enough data to positively identify the bear," Jane intoned. Ian huffed, exasperated.

"Identify her accurately yourself, then, Jane. She's at the holding facility. I told Frank we would be down as soon as possible, anyway. She needs to have her vitals checked, and I suspect she needs some treatment for malnutrition. I want to examine her while she's still unconscious, so I'm going immediately. Are you coming?"

What an odd expression she has on her face, thought Ian. Jane's face had layers. The surface of her face remained an impassive mask, but her eyes were bulging and they contained some degree of insanity.

"The Alert Program has its own veterinarian. My services are not required in this instance," said Jane.

"Oh for the sweet love of all that's sacred, Jane!" Ian exploded. "Aren't you even curious? Put your antipathy toward Anne out of your head for five minutes. Forget that the bear is special to her! This is a particularly at-risk animal we've been following closely for over a year. It's not playing favourites!"

He gathered equipment that he thought would be useful or helpful. Jane returned to her computer station and appeared to become engaged in what was displayed on the screen. Ian knew better. He could feel the hot magma bubbling below her surface. If Anne were here, she would either be freaking out about Tlingit or throttling Jane, thought Ian; she would probably be doing both.

His seat belt was secured and he was in the process of putting the CNSC's truck into reverse when Jane exited the front doors of the centre and walked directly to his vehicle. She opened the passenger door, slung her backpack onto the bench seat, got inside, and then stared directly ahead without acknowledging Ian. He suppressed the urge to grin and crack a joke.

Frank Hobbes met them in the foyer of the holding facility.

"Hurry. Stu wants to assess her and then wake her as soon as he can. She's underweight, so the anaesthetic really walloped her."

They proceeded to the examination room, where the bear lay unconscious on an expansive stainless steel surface. The room was equipped with a hydraulic lift. The stainless steel platform lay flush with the floor to allow for the easy transport of the animal's bulk. The platform could then be activated and raised for optimum examination of—and occasionally surgery on—the bear in question.

"She's used about all of her fat stores," said Stuart without preamble. "At two-hundred-ninety-eight pounds, she's on the light side of the light side. Nothing else is particularly wrong with her as far as I can tell. She's been in her fair share of scraps I would say. Quite a distinctive scar on her muzzle."

"Her name is Tlingit," said Jane. Ian raised an eyebrow. "She lost a cub in the springtime. The cub drowned. Tlingit exhibited unusual behaviour, including some vocalization that was hitherto unrecorded. The vocalization gave the impression of expressing the emotion of grief or loss. It appeared to be a reaction to the loss of her cub. These behaviours were duly recorded and they are currently the subject of a study being researched by our intern Anne McCraig." Jane cleared her throat.

"Thank you, Doctor Minoto," said Ian gently.

Jane's eyes became slightly fluid. "Let's proceed," she said.

Tentatively at first, Ian moved forward. She was a small female—the smallest adult bear he had ever seen—but her majesty and power were impressive all the same. The great black pads on her paws were twenty-five centimeters across so that she could distribute her weight on the ice. There was a thick curvature to her claws. Her shoulders were muscular and round. Her mandible was one smooth long line. These animals were capable of great violence, he knew. They were not just capable—it was their way of life. Nature, red in tooth and claw, thought Ian. She could kill and consume a beluga whale, and she probably had at some time in her life.

But she was also capable of tenderness, affection, and playfulness. He moved around to her great lolling head and smoothed the fur between her ears. He indulged the irresistible urge to push his fingers through the deeper, whiter fur of her neck. It was oily, coarse, and surprisingly tough. From a distance they look like plush toys, thought Ian. Each individual hair is not white but transparent and hollow. Each one is a tiny air-warming capsule. The skin underneath is black so that it can capture and retain heat. It is the perfect design for this environment.

Up close like this, she didn't have the appearance of a starving animal. There was just so much of her. Stuart was busying himself with the calipers, measuring the fat of her belly and then that of her shoulders. These bears needed a substantial supply of fat to survive the lean months, and from the tsk-tsk noises Stuart was making as he worked, Ian surmised that Tlingit's supply was insufficient, as Anne had thought.

"May I ask for five fifteen-cc syringes of blood?" asked Jane. She stood closer to the wall than she did to the bear, and she was almost immobile. Stuart nodded and exited the examination room, leaving Ian and Jane alone with Tlingit.

"Touch her," said Ian.

"It isn't necessary," Jane answered.

"Not all of our actions should be necessary, Dr. Minoto. Painting a picture isn't necessary. Listening to music isn't necessary. The human experience provides us with opportunities, and this is an opportunity for you and me. Life is short. Don't miss out."

With her lips pressed together tightly and her shoulders contracted, Jane Minoto approached Tlingit. She reached out her small hand and placed it flatly on the bear's topmost foreleg. Her eyes widened. Ian stepped backward and Jane took his place close to the bear's head. Amused, Ian watched as Jane struggled at first and then gave in and sunk her hand into the fur at the bear's neck. She breathed in involuntarily and deeply.

Full of the earthy, exotic scent of the bear, the air in the examination room was charged with some sort of presence, thought Ian. Inflated by the experience of touching this bear, the shape of an untold story ballooned up from Jane. It loomed over all of them. It undulated and asked to be told.

Stuart re-entered with the syringes. Jane yanked her hand away from Tlingit, stepped backwards, and assumed her clinical distance.

"This bear requires proximity to natural food source and distance from human populations. She demonstrates an inability to thrive in her current location," Stuart spoke as he plunged a needle into the bear's haunch. The little plastic vial immediately filled with dark red fluid. He replaced the vial with another one. "For all of the reasons in our criteria, this bear must be relocated. She is light, but she shouldn't be fed in captivity lest she learn that we're her food source. We need to expedite her move. We'll have to take her farther north than Wager Bay because even there we can't be certain of the stability of the ice at this time of year. Frank says tomorrow is possible. Your presence and expertise would be welcome."

"Will she sleep until then?" asked Ian.

"No, no, no," said Jane disapprovingly. "It's dangerous for her to remain anaesthetized. Unfortunately for her, she will have to experience a night of confinement here." Stuart nodded in agreement.

"Hey, what do I know? I'm just the plant guy," said Ian.

Gilbert

"Hey, Dad, how are you?" Charlotte called from Terrace every day to report on the status of her imminent blessed event, the arrival of his next grandchild, and to ask how he was doing. The sympathy in her voice was like too much maple syrup on pancakes.

"I'm fine, daughter. I just spent another day skimming oil off the river."

"Oh, Dad, that's horrible! What about the spirit bear?" He had told Charlotte about the search for the bear with oily paws.

"Gary hasn't seen him yet. He flies for an hour every day but still there's no sign. If Moksgm'ol doesn't want to be found, he won't be."

"Do you still have your house guests: the polar bear lady and the grizzly boy?" Charlotte asked. Gilbert paused and listened to the laughter coming from his garden. Anne and Jonathan were harvesting squash and kale.

"Yes. Anne and Jonathan," said Gilbert, careful to keep his voice sounding even. "Jonathan's almost well enough to come out and help with the cleanup. He cooks and he cleans.

Pretty good guest." He neatly avoided mentioning Anne, in case Charlotte could intuit the nightly sighs of pleasure, the urgent touching, and the kissing of soft lips in the evening that gently dissipated the dark images of the day.

"What about Max?" Charlotte asked.

"Things are busy for him at the tire shop," Gilbert said, not precisely fibbing but avoiding the truth for Charlotte's sake. "Haven't seen much of him."

Well, he hadn't seen much of Max—that much was true. The fact was, Max had never approved of his father's ardent activism against the pipeline project. He had been more a less a proponent of the thing, much to Gilbert's disgust and dismay. It was not a surprise, though—not really. His son had always rebelled against what Max had called "the headdress headspace," which meant the public touting of the traditional values of the First Nations.

"You're living in the past, Dad," Max had said again and again before the pipeline was constructed. "Money makes the world go round now. Natural resources make money. There's no use sticking your head in the sand. You can't turn back the clock and stop driving. You can't paddle everywhere in a canoe, and heat your house with wood alone."

"I heat my house with wood," Gilbert would say.

"Your tiny cabin. Nobody lives the way you do anymore, Dad."

"I live the way I do, Max."

"Yeah, well, most people don't. You've got your truck. You drive around. Everybody needs fuel. There are going to be lots more jobs in Kitimat and lots more people moving here. Everyone's going to benefit. If you want to go back to living in a longhouse, hunting, and fishing, then dig in. Don't hang around Kitimat whining about the pipeline though. The rest of us need the work."

Gilbert had countered with fiscal facts he thought his son would appreciate. The number of permanent jobs created by the pipeline was an insignificant handful, particularly compared with the thousands of jobs in recreation and adventure tourism that would cease to exist in the event of a spill. Canada would enjoy a meagre portion of the proceeds compared with the wealth that the pipeline would generate for the wasteful, distant purchasers of raw fuel. Gilbert tried to impress upon his son the priceless nature of the ecosystems which were put at risk because of the pipeline.

"That's if there's a spill," Max would reply. "Pipeline technology isn't what it used to be. You guys are like a bunch of Chicken Littles running around chirping that the sky is falling. The sky isn't likely to fall, Dad."

But the sky did fall. When it did, Gilbert felt no desire to call his son and say, "I told you so." Privately, every day of the cleanup he was hoping and half-expecting to see Max walking toward him on the oily beach, rolling up his contrite sleeves to lend a hand. Things were not—things were never—busy at the tire shop. It would have been a brave and moral thing for Max to show up at the cleanup.

This was unlikely, though. Max had never liked to do more work than was absolutely necessary. The boy was indolent by nature. It was not a wonder that Max considered selling the gifts freely given by the Creator a desirable road to riches.

Still thinking about Max, Gilbert said goodbye to Charlotte.

He remembered clearly the time, many years ago, when he had asked Max to help with stacking the firewood. Storm clouds were bearing down on Kitimat that afternoon. Clara and Charlotte had gamely agreed to abandon their own pursuits to get the big pile of wood he had split stacked while it was still dry. How old had Max been? Perhaps he had been eight years old—or nine—sitting in the gravelly sand of the driveway playing with his little metal cars.

"Max, come help your dad put this wood away."

"No!"

Gilbert had felt frustrated and a little angry, but he had recognized that this was a teachable moment, so he mastered his feelings and left his wife and daughter to stack firewood while he squatted beside his son.

"I'm going to tell you a story, Max. Would you like that?"

"Sure."

Moksgm'ol Teaches a Lesson

I t was autumn and there was much work to do to prepare for winter. There was meat and fish to smoke and preserve, berries to harvest, clothing to make and to repair. All the people of a village were happily working together, singing songs, telling stories, and laughing. No one noticed the one young man, Taaku, who wasn't contributing at all. He was not even collecting firewood, which was the favourite job of his peers. Taaku was sitting on a rock by the estuary, throwing stones into the water and brooding angrily.

Taaku saw a seal swimming alone in the water, rolling casually and lazily from back to front. The seal's glossy black fur glimmered in the sunshine, and his whiskers twitched happily. Look at Seal, Taaku thought, relaxing and doing as he pleases. No one is asking him to gather wood or gut fish or clean hides to make winter cloaks. I wish I could be Seal, he thought. Then he said the words he was thinking out loud, again and again.

"I wish *I* could be Seal. I wish *I* could be Seal."

Moksgm'ol, the spirit bear, was nearby listening to Taaku speak. The spirit bear had special powers given to him by the Great Bear, and he decided to use them now. Moksgm'ol turned the young man into a seal.

At first Taaku was delighted. He flexed his new lithe body in the water, diving down farther and longer than he had ever dared to dive as a human. He rolled on the surface, immensely enjoying the coolness of the water and the freedom of his new aquatic milieu. He grew bold and began to splash at the surface of the water. He let out happy barks, speaking to his friends on the shore, "Look at me! I have no chores to work on! I can play in the water all day!" Taaku splashed and barked, trying to attract the attention of the hard-working people of his village.

Instead, Taaku caught the interest of a hungry orca whale. He saw the big black dorsal fin slicing through the water toward him, and he began to swim away as quickly as he could. It was no use. The orca whale was gaining on him. He swam toward the shallows, hoping to enter water that was too shallow for the great black and white whale. As he approached the shore, he saw an eagle soaring high above the trees on the shore. Immediately, he fervently thought:

"I wish I were Eagle! I wish I were Eagle!"

Moksgmʼol was still watching from his place in the forest, and he decided to have some more fun. In a flash, Taaku ceased to be a seal and was instead an eagle, soaring high above the treetops and looking down on the black back of a confused and disappointed whale.

"Ha ha!" screamed the young eagle-man. "No one can touch me now, for I have no predators. I fly, free and unfettered, far above my village! Look at them all, slaving away down there, while I have the wind under my feathers and not a care in the world!"

Taaku the young eagle-man soared above the trees for a day and a half. The people of his village wondered and

worried about his absence. He laughed his shrill screaming laugh at them from high above. It wasn't long, though,
before he became lonely. He tried to talk to other eagles, but
they ignored him completely or chased him away. Once the
loneliness began, it became a painful ache. Taaku longed for
company. He looked down and saw a herd of black-tailed
deer standing in a clearing and feeding together. His heart
was breaking at the sight of so much camaraderie and he
expressed his longing:

"I wish I were Deer! I wish I were Deer!"

And then he was a deer, running over the fields and
through the forests, surrounded by other deer. He hooked
his small antlers with those of the other young bucks, tossing his head, playing, and testing his strength. At night he
slept with the herd, and he was warm and heartened by the
companionship. He grew smug as he remembered all of the
tasks that had to be accomplished by the people of his village. Taaku the young deer-man spent his days eating and
wandering idly through the forest.

Winter arrived with its coldness and snow. One day Taaku
wandered too far from the herd and found himself face to
face with a hungry black bear. The bear stood on its hind
legs and snarled its displeasure. Taaku tried to run away. The
hungry bear was right behind him though. It was so close
that the bear's hot breath reached the young deer-man's black
tail. Taaku couldn't think of any other creature to become
other than his pursuer, so he wished:

"Make me Bear! I want to be Bear!"

Moksgm'ol's powers were strong and the spirit bear had cast a lasting spell on the discontent young man. Immediately, Taaku became a young bear-man who looked like all of the black bears of the world. Mightily amazed and confused, the bear that had been pursuing him in his deer form ran away in the direction from which he had come. Taaku the newly formed bear immediately felt pangs of hunger in his bear-belly, and he followed his nose toward the good smells of smoked meat and fish that were coming from the Village of Men nearby.

As he approached the village, Taaku realized that it was his own village. He came through a thicket and abruptly came upon the most beautiful young woman of his village. She was carrying a basket into the forest to collect fuel for the fire because not enough fuel had been collected for such a cold winter. Taaku was torn by his twin desires. He wanted to eat the young woman and thereby assuage his hunger, but he also wanted to kiss her and court her because of her beauty.

The young woman saw Taaku's bear-form, and she dropped her basket. She was fierce and brave, though. She did not run from him; she faced him with impunity. His human heart was won by her courage and he once again implored the air around him:

"I wish I were a Man once more. I wish I were a Man!"

Then Moksgm'ol took pity on Taaku and gave him back his human form. The young woman was surprised. She gasped and she blushed because the young man had a tall, lean, and strong body and a handsome countenance.

"What are you doing so far away from your village?" Taaku asked. "It is a cold winter and the bears are hungry. It is dangerous to wander around alone!"

"There is insufficient firewood for my village, as we were shorthanded in the autumn and not enough fuel was collected, not enough meat was smoked, not enough warm clothing was made, and not enough fruits of the earth were harvested. Elders and babies are ailing. Those of us who can gather food and fuel must do so to save our village."

Then Taaku finally saw the error of his ways. He understood how lazy he had been. He understood how his family had suffered because of his indolence. He returned to his village with the young woman, and every day for the rest of that winter he collected fuel and hunted. Taaku was rewarded for his efforts with the respect of his village community and the love of the beautiful young woman.

"What did you think about that story?" Gilbert had asked his young son all those years ago.

"Bad," Max had answered. "You're just trying to make me do stuff I don't want to do. And I don't like girls. They're yucky."

Back in the present day, Gilbert's door banged open and he was snapped out of his reverie. Jonathan—that well-meaning, incompetent, enthusiastic, champion and defender of the natural world, thought Gilbert—entered the cabin carrying an armful of acorn squash. Red-cheeked and smiling, Anne was right at his heels, her arms full of dark-green, crinkly kale.

"Hey, guess what these squash remind Anne of?" said Jonathan. "Three guesses. You're never going to get it. It's so weird. It's not what you think, by the way."

"UFO's, her mother's meatloaf, other squash," said Gilbert.

Jonathan's jaw dropped. "Oh my God, you got it! These squash remind Anne of other squash!" Anne was giggling. She was beautiful, thought Gilbert. She was vibrant and passionate.

The three of them had fallen into a routine so easily. They had become a little impromptu family unit. Jonathan's wounds were more severe than he let on. Gilbert caught him wincing and limping when he thought no one was watching. The young man took his pain medication with dinner, and he fell asleep on the couch each night shortly thereafter, leaving Gilbert and Anne to sit out on the porch, where they would reflect on the day and enjoy their new romance.

"What's the story with your colleague?" Gilbert asked that evening. Anne had promised to convince Ian to bring his skills of botanical expertise and marksmanship to what the media were now referring to as "The Kitimat Oil Disaster."

"I emailed him this morning," Anne answered, yawning. "I'm afraid I resorted to guilt-tripping to get him on a plane. We'll find out soon enough if it worked."

Anne's email

Dear Ian,

I hope this finds you in good health and reasonably content. When I think about you, which is often, I imagine you attempting to engage with Doctor Jane 'Robot' Minoto, reading her desiccated reports and reaching her sad, flat little conclusions (Hmm, I can be condescending and judgemental from a distance, too! And bitter—did I mention bitter?).

How are 'our' bears? Naturally I wonder (and worry) mostly about Tlingit, but I would like a full report on all of them. And I would like to know about how much ice is forming in the bay and how much bog you've lost to fen. I did receive the group email with the weekly reports and the totals attached, but I don't currently have the leisure to analyze the data. I'm hoping you have both the time and the inclination, dear Ian, to write me a human version that will shed some light on this dispassionate document.

You must be wondering how bad it really is out here and whether or not the media reports you're reading and hearing about are accurate or whitewashed. The answer is the latter, of course—not by virtue of any cover up or corporate bribe but through sheer human bloody optimism and Pollyanna ideas about ecosystemic resilience.

"For example?" you might say. Aha! Gotcha! I heard you say it before you even had time to think it! You are a good scientist, Ian, and you need your proof.

When you hear that the spill occurred in 'downtown' Kitimat it is no exaggeration. For better or for worse, the pipeline ruptured in what can only be defined as 'downtown' Kitimat. My belief is that any benefit to the rupture occurring here and not in any remote wilderness between the British Columbia coast and the Alberta tar sands—quick emergency response, ease of mobilization and housing of cleanup crews are a few benefits being touted by Elba Energy—ignores two glaring negatives, to wit:

(a) *The spill was caused by human development, and therefore it didn't occur in a remote area. Humans fiddle and meddle and cause trouble. Sure, a landslide or other natural disaster could cause a rupture in the middle of nowhere, but is it likely? Historically, pipeline breaches and oil spills are caused by human error.*

(b) *A marine spill was always the ecologically worst-case scenario and— though it happened on land—this is a marine spill.*

For example, Ian, there are reports that the booms currently in place on the Kitimat River are preventing oil from reaching the much more sensitive, rife-with-vulnerable-marine-species

Douglas Channel, which leads eventually to the open ocean. In actual fact, plenty of oil either already got past or is getting past the booms. It might be through ground leaching or perhaps it had flowed into the channel before the booms were placed. But it's there.

Evidence? Yes I have hard evidence, Ian. My host, Gilbert, and I went for a hike along the southern shore of the Kitimat River estuary several kilometers west of Kitimat town center, where the spill occurred. The estuary has its share of grand and glorious coastal trees—your western hemlock, Sitka spruce, and giant cedar—but I was unprepared for the massive, lush meadows. The soil here is immensely nutrient-rich and it supports flowers. Well, I'm attaching a photo, as words fail. I can write 'spiky red flowers, tender descents of tiny yellow and white blossoms, tall stands of bold lavender' and so on. But you truly must see it to appreciate its wild, natural intense beauty. I would use the word 'unspoiled' to describe this ecosystem, but Gilbert and I found oil-asphyxiated birds and fish on the shore. Both on the surface of the water and onshore, oil residue is visible to the naked eye well past the booms that are supposedly containing the spill.

So there it is in the food chain. The shellfish, the orcas, the humpback whales, the sea lions, the seals, the black bears, the grizzly bears, the spirit bears, the eagles, the great blue herons, the trumpeter swans, the snow geese—this Alberta crude will make its slow, insidious way into their bodies, where it will wreak its irreversible havoc. As you and I know, the worst environmental disasters are not the volcanic eruptions, the tidal waves, or the earthquakes. Big, obvious natural calamitous events like that cause the most fatalities and damage to humans, their buildings, their houses, and their infrastructures. But the worst environmental disasters unfold at the majestic, stately pace of nature, spreading themselves quietly over generations. Just think about the receding ice shelf, which will move in tiny increments, just a little farther each year, until polar bears drown attempting to reach it.

Elba Energy is paying the cleanup crew, and although some people—mostly city folk—are volunteering and refusing to accept a dime from Elba Energy, many more people are delighted at this opportunity to make some extra cash.

I spent a morning hosing off rocks on the shores of the river with about fifty other people. I looked around and wondered if and why I was the only person ready to scream, "This is impossible! Can't you see that this place will never, ever be the same? Impossible!"

Take a jar of white sugar to a sandy beach. Pour the contents of the sugar jar onto the sand, distributing it over several square meters. Now pick up all of the sugar, grain by grain. And oh, did I mention that it's raining on that sandy beach? *The cleanup effort stretches off endlessly into the future. Ordinarily this would depress me, but fortunately for me I need to do something concrete. There's a* bear *in trouble, and Ian, I need your help.*

Gilbert Crow, my aforementioned host, is a kind of spirit-bear whisperer. He watches them and communes with them. Witnesses say a spirit bear that had been hanging around Kitimat was physically trapped by the cleanup effort, and it startled workers by running right through their midst in order to escape. The bear's paws, which are usually off-white, were stained black with oil. Gilbert says he knows this particular bear, and he's determined to find and relocate it. I'm going to lend my expertise to this endeavour and check the bear's vitals after it gets anaesthetized and during transport. I am going to outfit the poor thing with a transceiver so that we can monitor its progress afterwards and so on.

Unfortunately, the best marksman I know—the best hand with a dart gun—isn't here to lend his considerable skills to the effort. Ian, I really need you out here. As much as I'm reluctant to admit it, Jane's biochemical expertise would be a boon as well. A prompt hemobiographical analysis would tell us if and how badly the bear has been affected by oil toxins.

Best, Anne

Jonathan

It's midmorning in the cosy little Kitimat cabin. Gilbert and Anne, who in Jonathan's opinion are just about the coolest adults on the planet, left hours ago for another day of cleaning up oil. They return late in the afternoon each day, sweaty from exertion. They shower and then relate the day's activities over dinner prepared by Jonathan. So far they have washed beaches, transported stricken birds, shovelled up oily wood chips in the forest, spread fresh chips, and acted as crewmembers on boats siphoning oil from the Kitimat River. Jonathan longs to be out there with them, where he would become the eco-warrior of his imagination. His injuries from the bear attack are slow to heal, though. In spite of a course of antibiotics and gobs of topical ointments, the lacerations on his right thigh became infected, causing a painful setback to his recovery.

He doesn't like cooking, particularly. It was fun at first, though, creating salads from the late-season abundance in Gilbert's vegetable garden. So far he has only made two different meals: spaghetti and salad, and salmon and salad. He makes these two dishes on alternating nights to prevent boredom. Gilbert and Anne haven't complained. They are in love, Jonathan sees. It's his first close-up, real-life experience watching two people in love. He and his siblings never witness such love in his parents' marriage. Gilbert and Anne's behaviour reminds him of scenes from romantic films he has seen: extra-long starry-eyed gazing, impulsive hair tousling, and holding hands when they go for a walk for the entire duration of the walk. It's not uncomfortable for Jonathan. He doesn't feel like the third wheel. He doesn't feel like he is turning the cosy couple into an awkward crowd. Anne and Gilbert seem to genuinely enjoy his company. Anne flexes her as-yet untested maternal muscles, gently instructing him about the best way to poach an egg or sweep a floor.

Gilbert's demeanour around Jonathan leans more toward the professorial than the paternal. Twice, Jonathan has limped through the forest behind the cabin with Gilbert. The last time they did this was just yesterday. They followed the path down to the rocky shores of the river. In a couple of places, the younger man accepted the older man's help climbing over logs and negotiating slippery slopes. Now it is firmly the season of autumn. The sun has much less heat to offer. The sky is a paler blue. Grey clouds scud in off the ocean from west to east with menacing intent.

"You should know about the environment you're hoping to sustain," Gilbert had said. "This plant," He had said, kneeling down beside a thorny stem surrounded by broad, flat leaves, "is used by my people to treat certain skin conditions. The leaves are crushed and mixed with hot water to create a paste. It only grows in older forests."

At the river they had sat on a large, flat rock. Gilbert had told Jonathan about his people, the Haisla, which included the Kitimat, the "People of the Snow," and the Kitlope, the "People of the Rocks." He had told Jonathan about the Tsimshian People as well, the neighbours of the Haisla who share the same traditional social grouping system of the matrilineal clan.

"So, your family name comes from, like, your mother?" Jonathan's face had been a study in surprise.

"You bet," Gilbert had said. "The clans are Eagle, Beaver, Raven, Crow, Killer Whale, Salmon, Wolf, and Frog. I'm from the Crow clan, and my wife Clara was from the Frog clan. So, what do you think is important to my people?" Gilbert asked Jonathan.

"I think I get what you're saying," Jonathan had said. "White people have a totally different relationship with animals. I've got a story for you." Jonathan had told Gilbert the story of his grandfather, Lothar, and the Kolner Zoo, and he had told him about the firebombing of Cologne.

"Did all of the animals die?" Gilbert had asked.

"I guess so," Jonathan had answered. "I mean, they must have all died."

"That is a terrible story, Jonathan. Your grandfather's spirit was very sick. There was a disease of the spirit, then, in that time and place you describe—a contagious disease, I think. Many people caught it. Destroying the earth to make money is another contagious disease of the spirit. It has spread all over the planet. There are people who spread the disease on purpose—like some say the early European settlers did with the smallpox-infected blankets they gave to the Natives—but there are many others who inadvertently catch the disease from their parents and their friends."

"This oil spill is a symptom of the bigger disease. Humans talk about the economy as though it's something as real as this river that is running to the sea in front of us. But the economy could collapse—all of the money, real and imagined, could disappear tomorrow—and this river will keep running to the sea. Whether or not it runs clean and full of fish that we can eat and water that we can drink depends on how sick we are with the spiritual disease."

Jonathan is still mulling this concept over as he sits at Gilbert's desk surfing the internet the day after their conversation. The spectre of Nazi Germany in his ancestry has been weighing on him heavily since he learned of it. It helps to think about his grandfather as having a disease and not merely being a terrible person through and through. He researches the aftermath of the Firenight, the bombing of Cologne, but he is unable to find anything about what happened to the zoo animals that night. Then he types, "Happy the Panda, Kolner Zoo."

Jonathan eagerly reads that Happy had been purchased by a zoo in Saint Louis, Missouri, shortly after Cologne was bombed. The panda lived another few years in the Saint Louis Zoo and then died in 1946. As the grandson of Happy's captor, Jonathan is immeasurably cheered by this revelation. He passes the morning reading everything he can find about pandas in captivity. He learns about breeding programs, and he watches live streaming video of a mother panda cuddling her newborn at the San Diego Zoo. The video is a balm to Jonathan's spirit. It shows a big mama panda sprawled on her back and a tiny, perfect panda tucked sweetly in his mother's arms. Jonathan rests his head in his arms on Gilbert's desk and watches the video until he falls asleep himself. When he wakes up suddenly almost half an hour later, he has reddish squares on his left cheek— the imprint of the keyboard—and he discovers to his horror that he has drooled rather extensively onto the keyboard itself. He scrambles awkwardly to wipe the keyboard dry with his sleeve and this creates havoc on the monitor. I'm like a bull in a virtual china shop, he thinks to himself. He spends the rest of the morning staring at the monitor and clicking the mouse, returning Gilbert's desktop to its original state.

Dr. Jane Minoto

The evening meal consisted of a light salad of lettuce, apples, pine nuts, and olive oil; a pot of white rice fluffed with butter and salt; two whitefish filets quick-fried in a pan with garlic and herbs; and a bottle of crisp white wine. It was Ian's turn to make the evening meal. He whistled and bustled in the research centre kitchen, pleased with his manipulative tactics. These were Jane's favourite foods—not that she had ever discussed her preferences. Ian had learned about them through quiet observation.

They left the Polar Bear Jail, as the holding facility was colloquially known, before Stuart brought Tlingit back to consciousness. The bear would have to spend a night in a concrete cell. Stuart told them that she wouldn't know how fortunate she was. Many bears had spent weeks in this so-called jail before Hudson Bay froze over entirely and the bears could be released onto the ice. Ian and Jane agreed to meet Stuart and two other members of a bear transport team, including the helicopter pilot, at the holding facility at seven the next morning.

In the truck on the way back to the research station, Jane was a massive dam about to break. Ian could sense the water seeping through the stress fractures in the thick concrete of her restraining wall. Some comfort food will be good, thought Ian, along with a glass of wine, some caution, and some patience.

Later that night, as Ian contemplated the brilliant success of his plan, he made mental note of each step in his modus operandi, which he would employ at some later date. He had, of course, employed a similar technique trying to get women to have sex with him—always, though, with mixed results. Something about his timing and delivery had been perfect on this occasion, though the desired result was different.

He kept the conversation at the level of professional matters and light banter until they were both almost—but not quite—finished eating. He then topped off her wine glass and gave her a subtle compliment.

"I very much appreciated your professionalism today, Doctor Minoto." She had figured out, he was sure, that he meant the formal title as a term of endearment.

"Thank you," she said, her brown eyes widening. "It was a difficult day."

"Yes, it was. What happened, Jane? I mean, what happened in your past? What makes you so nervous?" Instead of looking directly into her eyes, Ian looked into his wine glass, swirling the pale liquid around and giving her time to respond.

There was a long pause. "Fine," said Jane shortly. "Fine." She took a large sip of wine and looked out the large picture windows of the dining area toward the blackness beyond.

"In 1941 my grandfather was placed in an internment camp in Greenwood, B.C. You have heard of these, yes?" Jane glanced at Ian, who nodded quickly.

"Heard of them, yes." said Ian. "I don't know much about them, though."

Jane continued to look out the window as she spoke. "As a knee-jerk federal reaction to the Japanese attack on Pearl Harbour, the Canadian government rounded up Japanese people in Western Canada and imprisoned them in camps, ostensibly to prevent sabotage and espionage. Living conditions in these camps were abysmal. Most of the detained lost all their possessions. Restitution for the families who were interned wasn't made until 1988."

"An embarrassing blot in Canada's history," said Ian.

"Yes," Jane agreed. "Before the camp, my grandfather had been a peaceful man who was content to fish by day and play cards by night. His wife, my grandmother, sold his catch in the market in Steveston, south of Vancouver. She was taken to the camp too with their oldest son, Akira, who was only five at the time. My father, Tomo, was born in the camp itself." Jane paused, closing her eyes. Ian kept quiet. "Afterward, my grandfather had changed. He was angry and very, very bitter. He taught his children to trust no one. He was strict to the point of being abusive. My father remembers cold showers every morning. He remembers being beaten for fraternizing with white kids. My grandfather allowed only the bare minimum of possessions in the house. He became paranoid about being stripped of his freedom at any moment."

"My father swore he wouldn't be like my grandfather. He allowed us, my sister and brother and me, to have the toys and clothes we desired. My mother honoured his wishes to keep our house furnishings simple, but we lacked for nothing—well, except for one thing. It was a frivolous thing. It was not a necessity but something we children all wanted very badly. We wanted a pet—a puppy." Jane swallowed. She grasped the edge of the table in front of her with both hands, bracing herself. Come on, Ian willed her in his mind. Let it out.

"My father said to us, 'we are absolutely not getting a pet and don't ask again.' Once my sister, after seeing a particularly charming cocker spaniel, asked him again if we could get a puppy. It was one of the only times my father ever struck one of us."

"I never fully understood the depth of my father's feelings on this issue. For him, caring for a non-human living creature was an ostentatious waste of resources. According to my father, my grandfather had felt the same way. I found out later that my grandparents had owned two dogs that they loved very much when they were taken away forcibly from Steveston and imprisoned in the internment camp. They never saw those dogs again."

"A schoolmate's mother arrived in the parking lot at my elementary school one day with a cardboard box. Inside the box was a litter of puppies. I don't know what breed they were. They were longhaired and black-and-white. They were free, by which I mean, there was no charge for them. This lady was giving away free puppies. I thought that if I brought one home, my father would fall in love with it and see how much joy it brought to his children. I thought that he would give in and let us keep it."

"You were wrong," Ian whispered.

"I was wrong," Jane confirmed. "My father was working a day job. We got home from school before him. We managed to hide Scooter—that's what I named him—in the backyard for two whole days before my parents became aware of him.

I don't know how my mother didn't figure it out before then. Scooter must have done nothing but eat and sleep all day while we were at school."

"On the third day, we ran home from school, giddy and excited to play with Scooter behind the house. When we got home, my father's car was parked in front of the house. For one tiny second I had the crazy hope that he was there to tell us we could keep Scooter. Then I saw my mother's face in the window. She was crying, which was something that she never did."

"The three of us ran around behind the house. My father was standing with a shovel in his hand next to a fresh pile of dirt. 'I told you,' he said, 'no pets.'"

Jane then wept in wracking spurts that jolted her entire body. Ian moved to her side and placed his long, strong hands over her delicate hands, which were still grasping the edge of the table. Her sobbing continued. Her shoulders were heaving. She snatched her hands away from Ian, raised them, and shoved Ian in an attempt to push him away.

"No," he said. "I'm not leaving you alone with this."

Jane stamped her foot in frustration and continued to cry, burying her face in her hands. "It was only a puppy!" she said in a muffled, wet voice.

"You loved it and he killed it," said Ian simply. Jane Minoto's contempt for Anne McCraig wasn't a mystery to him anymore. Anne's emotional devotion to Tlingit and her cub must have seemed immature and risky to Jane.

"Your father didn't quell your passion for animals, though, did he?" asked Ian as Jane's crying subsided to sniffs and the occasional sharp inhalation. "You still pursued a career in biology."

Jane sat up and cocked her head pensively. "My father is ashamed of me. He wanted me to be a medical doctor. I am a failure in his estimation."

"Excuse me, but if that is the case then your father is a fool. You are a huge success in the scientific field of your choice. You're brilliant, Jane. You must know how many applicants competed for these Churchill internships. You edged out— by an impressive margin, I understand—hundreds of your peers." Jane opened her mouth to reply, but Ian spoke over her. "Your work is accurate, insightful, and thorough. You're going to be a great asset in Kitimat. We should depart in seventy-two hours or as soon as possible after transporting Tlingit up north, as our mission in Kitimat is time-sensitive."

"Our mission? In Kitimat?" Jane shook her head, uncomprehending.

"Yes, Jane, our mission. I'm talking about the spirit bear that Anne urgently needs help relocating. Don't be coy. I know you've been following the newscasts as closely as I have been. This spill is a national environmental emergency. I've already spoken to the Arctic Research Institute and they are in agreement. We are suspending our research here in Manitoba to help out in British Columbia. We're staying at the Pacific Motor Inn in Kitimat. We're going to relocate the spirit bear and then complete an ursine risk assessment. I have estimated that it will take two weeks to collect the data. We can complete our report back here in Churchill in tandem with our polar bear research."

Ian created an inelegant stack of dishes. Though she was silent and immobile, he didn't wait for Jane to answer before he started striding to the kitchen. The crooked little smile on Dr. Jane Minoto's face informed him that she was on board with the Kitimat project.

Tlingit

This man-place is strange and hard. It is a strange, cold man-place. It is so foreign and so strange—a dream-yet-not-a-dream. It is a nasty dream—a nightmare. There is pungent man-stink in my fur. The light of man is coming from a small round ball above—not light of sun, not light of the Great Ball of Light in sky. It is man-light: blank, empty, and soulless.

I am numb everywhere—numb like the pads of my feet on the coldest day. This numbness is also inside my head, tingling and painful. Escape is impossible. Maybe I will wake up from this dream, this long bad dream of not enough ice, nothing to eat, no little K'ytuk. Am I imagining all of this? My hunger is now far away. Now the hunger is not as bad as the numbness.

I see the light of the sky coming from a square so high on the flat wall of the man-place. In front of me are the man-place lines—hard lines that are too small to push between and run away. I push my face between the lines, but my body cannot follow. I have no strength.

Man! A man comes to the place outside of the hard lines. My body moves slowly—too slowly. There is nowhere to run away! The man is standing so close that I could bite the man and taste his man-blood and eat the man, but it is not possible because of the hard lines. The man is speaking. The man is making man-noises—ah, man-noises over and over.

This box is a nightmare. The man outside of the box makes man-noises. First came no ice. Then came no cub, no K'ytuk—no baby. Too far, swimming too far to swim. Then there was no food—nothing for eating. Now there is numbness. Now there is no world of the bear.

Tlingit's Flight

The crooked little smile on Jane's face lasted through the night, and it was joined in the morning by a spring in the scientist's step. She toasted a bagel, smeared it with cream cheese and jam, and consumed it with an appetite that had hitherto been notably absent. She refilled Ian's coffee with a flourish. He smiled at his colleague, pressed his lips together, and thought of serious matters to keep from laughing outright. Her load was so visibly lessened that Ian thought he might have to tether her to keep her from floating like a helium balloon off into the stratosphere.

She kept watch out the window of the helicopter, craning her neck to keep the shape of Tlingit, who was dangling in a net, in sight. Ian didn't watch the bear but the watcher of the bear. Jane Minoto was evidently concerned and not dryly detached. She had foregone prior opportunities for going on relocation flights, but now Ian thought he understood her reluctance. All she needed was permission to care, thought Ian. Who is this person? Anne isn't going to recognize her.

The little white ball of fluff hung under the helicopter, swinging like a pompom on a strand of white wool. Buffeted by wind and velocity, this little white puff was the bear that Anne loved—the bear that had so loudly mourned the cub she lost to the icy waters. This was the same bear whose image surrounded them all—thanks to Anne—as they moved through the hallways of the research station. Tlingit was equipped with two transceivers, one in her skin and another in her gum line. They would be able to track her, monitor her progress, and assure themselves by her movements that she was alive and hopefully thriving in her new colder and more remote hunting grounds.

Having been lightly sedated and having had her eyes smeared with Vaseline to protect them from ice and wind,

Tlingit would be aware of her surroundings but nonplussed by them, Stuart had assured them. Undernourishment notwithstanding, her condition had been good prior to take-off.

Thirty-five minutes elapsed. With every kilometer of latitude gained, the ice in the bay below them seemed to magically thicken and increase until, just prior to making landfall, the line between shore and bay became indistinct. The pilot hovered over a flat, open area. Stuart, Ian, Jane, and Frank exited the helicopter. Frank unhooked the net from the line attaching it to the aircraft. The pilot moved his craft fifty meters away and landed.

A thin, icy snow was falling. There were billions of tiny sharp needles. They opened the net and each of them took a corner. Tlingit's eyes were unfocused as they flicked from human to human. She seemed aware of her predicament.

"She's scared," Jane observed.

"She doesn't have the energy to be scared," Stuart answered. "Come on. This will take all of us."

Jane looked skeptical. "He's done this dozens of times," Ian assured Jane. The bear had to be rolled off the net. Her great limbs flopped over uselessly as they all pushed and heaved her substantial bulk. Stuart controlled her head, ensuring that her neck wasn't injured. After two full rotations of her body, she was in the snow and free of the net. Frank folded the net for the return trip and walked toward the helicopter. Stuart extracted a green pen from his pocket and began to draw a large, distinct dot on Tlingit's head.

"I'm doing this so that the people of Nunavut will know she has the anaesthetic drug in her system," Stuart explained. He then took handfuls of snow and began to rub some snow into her fur. "Well, come on," he said when Ian and Jane didn't immediately participate. "Help me out here. This will remove some of our human scent from her fur and make her more comfortable when she comes out of it." Ian and Jane quickly followed suit, rubbing snow into the bear's thick fur.

They withdrew and stood about halfway between the bear and the helicopter. Within five minutes the bear began to lift her head and sway it from side to side, sniffing at her new surroundings. Ten minutes of sniffing and surveying passed. Then, with a gargantuan effort, Tlingit engaged her forelegs and pushed herself back onto her haunches.

"That's our cue," said Stuart brightly. "Back in the bird, everybody."

"I'd prefer to see her standing before we depart," said Jane, a little indignant.

"May I remind you how healthy her appetite is at present," Stuart said, amused. "You are the nearest source of sashimi. If you wait until she stands, it will probably be the last thing you ever do."

The force of the helicopter's rotors pushed the light, sparkling snow up into a cloud it as it took off. The pilot was cognizant of his passengers' desire to take a long and potentially final look at the polar bear propped up groggily on the ice below. He circled above her twice.

"She looks so lonely," said Jane.

"She looks so free," said Ian.

Ian's Reply

Dear Anne,

You had me at "There's a bear in trouble and I need your help." My flight leaves in the morning three days from now. I've booked a motel room in Kitimat. I'm attaching a list of equipment I'll require, but I'm leaving it up to you to round it all up.

Of course, as soon as you donned your spandex super-scientist suit and flew off to high adventure on the Western ocean, things got interesting around here. It's been an eventful few days. I'll fill you in when I get out there. Jane—and you really ought to be more charitable, Anne—has been extraordinarily helpful.

See you soon, my friend.

Ian

Convergence

With a sigh of brakes and an engine cough, Gilbert and Anne arrived home from another day of work at the spill site. The young hippie from Vancouver met them at the door more dishevelled than usual, wearing an apron smeared with a variety of foodstuffs.

"I hope there's a pizza joint in this town," Jonathan yelled from the porch as Anne stepped out of the truck, "because there's nothing edible for us here. This woodstove is crazy, man. It burns everything. And you're out of dish soap." His eyes bulged from his face, which was sweaty with exertion.

"Cabin fever," Gilbert whispered to Anne, winking conspiratorially.

"You haven't had a proper tour of Kitimat, have you Jonathan?" Gilbert shouted from the driver's seat. His voice was kind and jovial. "There are not one, not two, but three pizza places in this town. Leave that apron on the porch and let's you and me go for a drive."

Jonathan pulled the apron over his head and dropped it where he stood, descending the porch steps by hopping on his right leg and holding the handrail. He limped furiously past Anne, shaking his head and muttering, "Sorry about the mess."

Anne showered and donned fresh, clean clothes before putting the cabin's kitchen back into some semblance of order. Somehow, the young man had managed to dirty half the dishes available to him without producing a meal. Anne returned an egg carton containing three eggs and an ancient, shrivelled piece of ginger root to the refrigerator. She took a bowl of coffee grounds, eggshells, and wilted lettuce outside to the compost pile. Scraping a frying pan surface with steel wool, she reflected on how satisfying these domestic chores were compared to the ineffectual nature of the work at the oil spill site. As far as Anne could see, the days were passing without any appreciable lessening in the quantity of oil washing up on the shores of the Kitimat River. The number of compromised birds and fish pulled from the polluted water wasn't growing any smaller. Earlier in the day, Gilbert had inspired her not to lose heart.

"The earth is strong. She wants to breathe and recover and live and thrive," he had said. Looking into Gilbert's eyes, which were dark with sincerity and conviction, Anne's faith was restored a little. "Being discouraged won't siphon the oil off of the beach or make ice form in the Arctic," he had said. "It won't bring anything or anyone back to life. We only have today—now, this moment—as imperfect as it is. That's what Clara taught me."

"She was a special woman," Anne had said.

"She was special. You're special. I'm a lucky man," Gilbert had answered, bringing a rosy blush of colour to Anne's fair cheeks.

Gilbert and Jonathan had been gone for a quarter of an hour when Anne's cell phone rang.

"Anne! It's Ian. We just arrived at the airport here. I had no idea it was so far outside of town. Any chance you can come pick us up and take us to our motel?"

"Ian! You aren't supposed to be here until tomorrow! And who is *we*?" asked Anne.

"I got the date wrong, sorry! And I'll explain when you get here."

"Sorry, Ian, but I don't have access to a vehicle. Walk outside the building and look for a big, tall First Nations man with glasses. His name is Little Ted and he drives a cab. I'll text you his phone number in case he isn't there. Where are you staying?"

"Pacific Motor Inn," answered Ian. "I'm walking outside the airport. Oh okay. That guy you described with an oxymoron for a name is here. Thanks, Anne. When will we see you?"

"Gilbert and I will come to your motel this evening. Text me your room number once you've checked in, okay? And who is *we*?" Anne thought that she might catch Ian off guard.

"Nice try, Anne. I'll see you this evening."

"Oh, Ian!" An opportunity for mischief occurred to Anne. "Tell that cab driver—Little Ted, make sure it's him—tell him that you and I were engaged and that you're here to win me back from the man who has stolen my heart."

"Having a little fun, are we, Anne?" Ian asked. "Are you sure? This guy looks like he might have a heart condition."

"I'm sure."

Three hours later, Gilbert and Anne arrived at the Pacific Motor Inn. They had intended to bring along their young injured housemate, but Jonathan, who was full of painkillers and pizza, was asleep before they left, curled up in his sleeping bag on the floor of the cabin. A red neon sign on a rusty iron post revealed the location of the motel. The dilapidated building slumped behind a neglected parking lot where weeds were growing out of multiple cracks and potholes in the asphalt. Gilbert parked in front of a mottled brown door with the number fourteen inexpertly painted on it in white. Little Ted's taxicab was parked in front of room number twelve.

"I wish I had more room at my place for your friends," said Gilbert. "This motel is a little rundown."

"I don't know who or how many people Ian has with him," Anne replied. "And you're already the Hospitality Hero, Gilbert. Ian will make do." They leaned toward each other in the cab of the truck and kissed.

The door to number fourteen swung open. Gilbert and Anne pulled apart and dismounted from their respective sides of his truck. Little Ted was the first to emerge from the motel, prompting Gilbert to raise a quizzical eyebrow. From behind the cabbie's great bulk, a second person slid out. Anne recognized the slight form of Dr. Jane Minoto. The cheerful, welcoming smile on Jane's face caused Anne to experience a moment of surrealism-induced vertigo. Finally, ducking to avoid smacking his head on the low doorframe, Ian emerged.

He stretched up to his full height and opened his arms in a loving, conciliatory gesture.

"Honey," Ian addressed Anne, "I'm here."

"I didn't know, Gil," said Little Ted, cringing at the confused look on his friend's face.

"What is *she* doing here?" Anne addressed Ian. The tentative happiness playing about Jane's lips began to wobble precariously.

"What didn't you know, Ted?" Gilbert asked the cab driver.

"They," he indicated Ian and Anne with a swoop of his arm, "were engaged once. I had no idea. I wouldn't have complicated your life knowingly Gil. She," Little Ted pointed a big finger accusingly at Anne, "broke it off."

All eyes were on Gilbert Crow. It was twilight on a crisp, cool October evening. They stood in an awkward oval under tiny pinpoints of light in an indigo sky. A chorus of frogs croaked somewhere nearby. A raven flew overhead, low enough that its wing-beats were audible. It pushed evenly into the night air.

"I believe," began Gilbert slowly, "that the joke is on you, Ted." Ian grinned. "We haven't known each other for very long, but I'm certain of two things: I love Anne," said Gilbert. "She loves me. And you," he addressed Ian and reached out a hand toward the botanist, "must be Ian. Anne respects you very much." The men shook hands formally and respectfully.

"And you," Gilbert turned to Jane. The little woman's lips were trembling violently. She was clenching and unclenching her fists.

Jane turned and ran away at a brisk clip into the darkness.

"Go after her," Ian ordered Anne. Anne immediately obeyed, her heavy boots thumping on the pavement.

"Jane!" yelled Anne as she ran. "Wait up, Jane!"

Gary's cell phone rang. He turned his back and wandered away as he spoke, stopping at a slanted, rusty metal staircase leading up to the second floor of the motel.

Little Ted and Ian considered each other in silence.

"Sorry," said Ian.

"It's okay," said Little Ted. "I had it coming," He removed his glasses, squinted, and pinched the bridge of his bulbous nose. "Mom keeps telling me to keep this big-ugly thing out of other people's business."

"No hard feelings, then?" Ian offered a hand. They shook hands.

"None at all."

A reverberating metal clang resonated from the staircase and then another. *Clang, clang, clang.* Gilbert was knocking his head repeatedly on the rickety banister of the motel staircase and punctuating a rhetorical question.

"Why"—*clang*—"does everything"—*clang*— "happen" — *clang*—"at once?"

Gilbert stopped banging his head and ambled back to the rectangle of light cast by the open door of room fourteen. Ian and Ted looked at him expectantly. He considered both of them for some time before speaking.

"My daughter is in labour," said Gilbert eventually, "and the spirit bear's in town. It's going to be a long night."

"And an auspicious one," said Little Ted, indicating the northern sky. Long, erratic green and purple lines were leaping and swaying—a contemporary dance of heavenly scarves sprinkled with the sequins of stars.

"Wow," Ian gasped. "Spectacular."

The three men stood in mute appreciation with their heads cocked back, watching the increasingly dramatic display.

Six blocks away, Anne and Jane stood together on a residential street, having adopted a posture identical to that of the men. With their heads tilted back and their arms akimbo, they watched the ballet of light and movement in the northern sky. Jane had continued to run for some minutes, her head and heart in turmoil. Anne's plaintive calls were audible behind her, but once Jane had begun to flee it was difficult to stop. Jane knew she could easily have outrun her pursuer. The ridiculousness of running away from Anne soon made her ashamed, though, and she halted and turned around.

Red-faced and panting, Anne was incapable of speech. She staggered gratefully to a walk, lifted her arm, and pointed over Jane's head. Jane followed the direction of Anne's extended finger and her eyes widened. Her mouth opened in surprise.

They watched in silence for several minutes. The celestial show was increasing in its intensity. Without averting her gaze from the sky, Jane began to speak. She unfolded her traumatic childhood tale just as she had told it to Ian, but she did so without weeping this time. Anne more than made up for Jane's passionless delivery with an abundance of tears and horrified cries of, "No." Jane reached her story's dark conclusion and Anne impulsively wrapped Jane in a moist, crushing embrace.

"I'm so sorry Jane! Please, can you ever forgive me? I have been myopic in the extreme!" Anne wailed. "Why do I expect everyone to be like me and to react to things exactly the way I do? I have judged you so unfairly! Can you ever forgive me?"

Jane bore this onslaught of cathartic humility, and she even ventured a few reassuring taps on Anne's back. When she thought she could be heard over Anne's emotional release, she spoke up.

"Tlingit's up north of Wager Bay. I think she's going to do very well there."

"What?" Anne sniffed. "How did...?" She pulled back from her colleague, confused and furrowing her brow. Once again, Jane was obligated to narrate. Anne's interjections this time were direct and professional.

"How long was she anaesthetized? She was already compromised. Is she outfitted with transceivers?"

As they walked back toward the motel, Jane patiently answered Anne's queries in her accustomed way of using clipped, methodical, and precise details. The neon Pacific Motor Inn sign was half a block away when Gilbert's truck pulled up beside the two women. Gilbert put the truck in park, slid over, and opened the passenger door.

"Enjoying the light show? We'll be able to see it really well from Gary and Sandra's back deck. Hop in," he said.

Anne clambered in, slid over next to Gilbert, and then extended her hand to hoist tiny Jane into the truck's cab. "Gary and Sandra's? At this time of night? Should I ask why?" Anne wondered.

"You should not," Gilbert answered. "There's no point, really. Gary will explain things when we get there. Charlotte's in labour, by the way."

* * *

"I never did spot him from the air," Gary explained. "Burned a lot of fuel looking, though. He must have been hiding out somewhere or else the crew who saw him run got the direction wrong. Can't see him crossing the river again, filthy with crude oil as it is right now."

"I am so fucking angry. I've been angry for weeks!" Sandra interjected. "We knew there would be a goddamn spill. Ignorant money-hungry bastards! Poor bear." Her eyes were wild. Anne nodded at Sandra in sympathetic agreement. They stood outside, as Gilbert had predicted, watching the display of northern lights from a second-floor cedar deck that ran the length of Gary and Sandra's house. Gilbert gave perfunctory introductions and explained the impromptu meeting.

"I was on the phone with Walter, Charlotte's husband, when your call came in, Gary," said Gilbert. "Charlotte's in Terrace at her in-laws' place. Her water broke about seven o'clock. Walter's going to keep me updated. There's not much I can do. Walter's mother is monitoring her contractions. It's my daughter," Gilbert addressed Jane and Ian, who nodded their understanding.

"So," Gary took over the narration, "a spirit bear was seen just north of here this evening browsing on berries and pushing branches down to feed on them. The lady who saw him noticed that his paws were black and called the new Environment Canada number for reporting oil-damaged wildlife. The team there knows I've been looking for this bear, and they gave me a call. They have all the gear we need and a helicopter pilot standing by to transport the bear in the morning. I told 'em we've got a sharpshooter to do the tranquilizing—a specialist from Churchill. I take it that is you, sir." Gary regarded Ian seriously.

"I spent two years in the Royal Canadian Army Cadets with lots of success on the rifle range," Ian answered. "It's come in handy with the polar bears."

"Great. Let's go inside and have a look at the map," said Gary.

They filed inside and each of them took a final gaze at the colourful rippling lights in the northern sky. They had all witnessed this celestial phenomenon before, and they knew that the show could either continue for hours or stop at any time.

Gary spread out a map on the kitchen table. He jabbed a finger at a spot just outside of the municipality of Kitimat. "Here's the bear's approximate location. Bait has been dropped here, here, and here." Gary indicated a narrowing scalene triangle. "With the bear in this approximate area, we can move in along this road," he said, sweeping his finger along a line parallel to the Kitimat River, "and move him within range. The helicopter could put down within twenty or thirty meters almost anywhere along here."

"I'd like to help," said Sandra.

Gary nodded and smiled at his wife. "You and I can walk the east boundary. Anne and Jane can walk the west boundary. We'll take noisemakers and of course bear spray, though I know we won't need it. If this guy were aggressive, he would have attacked a few weeks ago when he was cornered. Gilbert, you can wait with the pilot and intercept this bear once he's got a tranq dart in him. Ian, you wait here," Gary said, tapping a spot on the map repeatedly, "at the tip of the funnel. If we're lucky, you'll have a good bead on him while he's on the road. We'll all be in radio contact all of the time. Channel three."

"Do we have confirmation that the bear is in fact a male?" Jane asked.

"We're drawing a conclusion based on size," Gary answered. "Now, Sandra and I don't have any experience slinging up bears and flying them around. Local expertise is limited. You four got all the know-how you need?"

"Ian and I assisted in a transport in Churchill three days ago," Jane said. "I'm confident we can safely transport this animal. Anne, is there anything we can do about the oil on his paws?"

"I've been researching it. Plain old detergent is the least toxic and most effective cleaner we can use. I'm going to work quickly once we land on Princess Royal Island and get as much off as I can before he comes around." Anne smiled warmly at Jane, and the latter responded in kind. Ian watched the exchange with a wry smirk.

"I feel all warm and fuzzy," he said. "Kind of like a bear."

"Oh hush," said Anne. "Gilbert, what about Charlotte?"

"She's having a baby," Gilbert said, sombrely. "I guess my friend Gary will fly me to Terrace once the Spirit Bear is safe and sound, seeing as how I'll be too tired to drive."

"I'll fly you," said Gary, "but just this once. I'm not going to renew my license next year."

"Why not?" Gilbert tilted his head, curious.

"I've got to stop burning fuel, man. As long as we keep burning it up, they're going to keep sucking it out of the earth." Gary shook his head sadly.

The Great Bear Creates the Aurora Borealis (Northern Lights)

The Great Bear created the earth and all of the bears of the earth. She created people and the other creatures of the earth. As she did these things, she wrote their stories in the stars. We can look up and read the stories of the Great Bear in the stars on any clear night, and on cloudy nights we know the stories are there, waiting to be unveiled and enjoyed as soon as the clouds disperse.

One day the Great Bear was walking in the sky, looking down at the earth she had created. On that day she looked to the east and saw a panda bear nuzzling a panda sow. The Great Bear looked more closely and saw that the female panda was pregnant with a cub. The panda male was solicitously ensuring that his mate was warm, nuzzling her tenderly to display his affection.

Then the Great Bear looked to the west and saw a grizzly mother catching fish and feeding them to her cubs. The Great Bear could see that the grizzly mother was hungry herself and wanted to feed, yet she fed her young cubs first and watched while they consumed the meal she had caught for them.

To the south, the Great Bear saw three black bears being threatened by a pack of wolves. One of the black bears was elderly; it certainly would not survive a wolf attack alone. The two younger bears moved to protect the older bear, blocking the wolves with their bodies as they stood on their hind legs and roared their terrible roars. The young bears stood up, snorted, charged, and stood up again until finally the wolves were dissuaded from their attack.

She finished her survey of the compass points with a look to the north, and there she saw a pair of one-year-old polar bears, a brother and a sister, playing with each other. They swatted each other gently, wrestling and rolling in a new carpet of fluffy white snow. When they needed to rest, they rested together. Each of them waited for the other to catch his or her breath before springing into play-action again.

The Great Bear saw these expressions of love everywhere she looked, and she was filled love herself. She was filled with a tremendous, expansive, and irrepressible joy. She did not contain this joy, but rather she expressed it to the great, beautiful world that she had made. Her joy came out of her in waves of light and colour, shimmering and spreading out over the skies. These displays of the Great Bear's love and joy are visible in the night sky as the northern lights, or the Aurora Borealis.

Jonathan

The sound of the wood-frame screen door banging open and closed woke Jonathan in what he first believed to be the middle of the night. As his eyes adjusted to the dimness, he watched Gilbert and Anne tiptoe past him into the little back bedroom of the modest cabin. It must be the very crack of dawn, he thought. Then he wondered where the heck his host and the blonde biologist had been, and he wondered what they had been doing all night.

He had retired early the night before, and now that he had woken up sleep was eluding him. He thought about how he didn't want to move back in with his roommates back in Vancouver. The floor of the city apartment was more often than not an obstacle course of stale ashtrays, rolling papers, and pizza crusts. It was impossible to invite a girl over without risking disdain at minimum, if not outright revulsion. He recalled the career-counselling session he had signed up for toward the end of his final year at university. Find a job in your field as soon as possible, the counsellor had said. But jobs in environmental sustainability were pretty thin on the ground.

"The bottle depot is hiring," one of his roommates had suggested. "You know, the recycling center. Counting people's empties—that falls into your area of expertise."

Jonathan hadn't deigned to answer.

Frustrated, he rolled over to his side. Placing one hand firmly on the arm of the couch, he sat up, yawning. He decided to walk—or more accurately, hobble—to the main tent of the spill cleanup effort. It couldn't be more than ten or fifteen minutes away by foot for an able-bodied person. He could be there in half an hour. He got dressed and consumed half a loaf of bread smothered with the better part of a jar of saskatoonberry jam pilfered from Gilbert's larder.

Traffic Control and Perimeter Security Guard was the title of his first job at the spill site, and it was not something Jonathan would ever dream of including in his resume. Elba Energy trucks were allowed past his checkpoint, as were police and emergency vehicles, oil pump trucks, and City of

Kitimat municipal vehicles. All other traffic was disallowed past Jonathan's rickety lawn chair and yellow tape barrier.

"Sorry," he had said to the driver of a shiny black SUV. "The road's closed. You can turn around half a kilometer up this road, here." It was perhaps the eighth or ninth vehicle he had seen in the three hours that had elapsed since he had started his shift. Gilbert had encouraged him to bring a book, and he had loaned him a small volume of local First Nations legends. Jonathan was grateful that Gilbert had insisted. He would spend eight hours sitting in the same spot, stopping one—maybe two—cars an hour. Still, Jonathan reflected, it beats spending another day hanging around the cabin peeling carrots.

He settled back down into the folding chair, a cheap made-in-China contraption that was developing a warp in one leg from Jonathan's attempts to make it into a recliner. Overhead, the sky was boiling. Grey shreds of storm clouds were surfing low under patches of light. There was white fog and he could see that the September sunlight, with its summer memories, had given way to October's serious, wintery intent. The surrounding mountainsides, carpeted mostly with conifers, had little splashes of yellow, orange, and red fall colours, betraying the locations of deciduous shrubs.

The roadside trees seemed to loom over him on this rainy day, and Jonathan noted the girth of the base of a large cedar a few meters into the forest. It looked like it was at least two meters wide at the base. Squinting, he saw more massive trunks further into the forest. They were noble giants. The branches swept down like mighty arms. He imagined Tolkien's Ents, ancient tree-people, yanking up their root-legs and walking majestically over mountains.

Jonathan took a deep breath, held it in, and exhaled slowly. The petroleum smells weren't noticeable here. He couldn't tell whether the forest was filtering them or the molecules had simply dissipated this long after the spill. This air was invigorating. It smelled like mud, ocean, and oxygen. It smelled like bark, spruce needles, and sap. He opened the book and riffled through its pages. There was a pen-and-ink illustration of trees; the species of tree was similar to that of the trees surrounding him, and the drawing caught his eye. He began to read.

The Three Sisters

Once there was a chief who had three daughters. As they became young women they all grew tall, and they were all beautiful and clever in their own ways. The elder two sisters became competitive with each other, vying for their father's attention. Each of them wanted to accompany their father alone on canoe journeys he made up and down the coast, for each of them believed that she would meet a desirable mate before the other two would, thereby proving that she was the most beautiful.

The eldest daughter lingered outside of her father's longhouse late one evening, eavesdropping on the conversation inside, and she learned that the next day her father would be departing early with a company of twelve people to visit another village to the south by canoe and trade with them. She went to the campfire and collected ash. She then sprinkled it on her sister's faces as they slept.

The eldest daughter did not sleep that night. In the morning, she went to the shoreline as the canoes were being readied for the journey and asked her father if she might accompany him on his trip.

"Ask your sisters if they would like to come as well," said the chief.

"Oh no, father," said the eldest girl. "They are too young. They play in the dirt all day and do not clean themselves. It wouldn't be diplomatic to take them."

"Well, let me see for myself," said the chief. He went to the longhouse where his younger two daughters were just waking up, and he called them outside. They appeared sleepily, their faces covered with ashes and soot.

"Ah daughters!" exclaimed the Chief. "Your sister will come with me to the next village, but you two cannot come, for you haven't washed your faces or combed your hair. You can come next time, perhaps."

The eldest sister was triumphant, and the younger two daughters were astonished. They looked at each other, saw the soot, and realized their sister had tricked them.

The eldest daughter did not meet a man to marry on that voyage. In another two moons, the middle daughter saw some elders preparing blankets one morning, and she asked what they were for.

"They are for your father's voyage to the next village to the north," answered her grandmother. "He departs in the morning, and we must hurry to finish these blankets."

The middle daughter saw her opportunity. She went to her sisters and told them that she had found an especially large and juicy crop of berries. She bragged that she would go to the crop at dawn the next day and harvest baskets and baskets of berries to present to the chief, who would then of course favour her. That afternoon she set out to the east, pretending to be surreptitious about her departure. Her sisters, of course, followed her to discover the location of the big berry patch.

After she had walked for some distance, the middle sister turned and ran back the way she had come, catching her sisters in the act of following her.

"Aha!" said she. "You thought you would steal the berries before I could harvest them myself. Well, I shall go no farther, and you shan't find the patch!"

Naturally the elder sister thought she could easily find the berry patch, and the next morning she rose early and set out in the same direction her sister had taken the day previous. The eldest sister woke the youngest sister, and insisted that the latter accompany her in the search for the berry patch.

The middle daughter, in the meantime, went to the shoreline and asked if she could accompany her father, the chief, on his voyage.

"Yes, you may," said he. "Let us ask your sisters if they would like to come along as well."

"Oh, no, father," said the middle daughter. "They could never be ready to depart in time. They have gone without your permission to visit their friends in the next village to the east. I implored them not to go, but they wouldn't listen."

Then the chief went to the longhouse, where his other two daughters should have been sleeping, and sure enough, they were not there. He embarked on his trip to the north with his middle daughter, but she did not meet a mate on this journey.

Many moons passed. Winter came with its coldness, ice, and biting winds. The chief did not make any trading journeys to other the villages while the storms were stirring up the ocean into waves as big as longhouses and as tall as totem poles. The elder two daughters exchanged many angry, jealous words while winter kept them home, but the youngest daughter was quiet and she kept her own counsel. The chief noted the difference in his daughters, and he reflected upon it.

Spring arrived with little birds singing, small flowers opening, and the sea growing calm. The chief gathered his village and announced that he would make a visit to the islands in the west for the first time. He would bring fine carvings, blankets, smoked fish, and meat. He would bring the finest items his village had to offer.

"Oh, take me. Take me!" shouted the eldest daughter.

"No, take me. Take me with you!" shouted the middle daughter.

"I shall take my youngest daughter," said the chief, and the eldest and middle daughters were stricken with remorse for they knew that their father the chief had thought carefully when he chose only the finest.

When the canoes returned three weeks later, they contained an extra passenger: a young man from the islands to the west who was tall, strong, and handsome. He had chosen the youngest daughter to be his bride. They were married in a ceremony on the shore that very spring.

In time the eldest and middle daughters got married also. They begged their father and their youngest sister for forgiveness for their vanity and pride. The three sisters became great friends and they bore many children, raising them together with laughter and love. As they grew old, they often walked together in the forest, telling stories, laughing heartily, holding hands, and facing each other in a circle. The Great Bear saw them doing this, and so pleased was she with the three sisters' journey on the earth that she turned them into trees. Today you can go for a walk and visit the three tall and beautiful sisters in the forest, where they are still holding hands and laughing amongst themselves.

It began to rain as Jonathan was reading the final paragraph of the legend. He hunched over the book, trying to protect it from water damage. A few big drops found their way through regardless, and he wiped at them with the sleeve of his jacket, forgetting that it too would be wet. The whole page was damp now and streaked with mud. Jonathan stood up in alarm, toppling his lawn chair.

"Oh, jeez. Sorry, Gilbert," he said to his absent host. The book had looked brand new a minute ago, but now it was irrevocably compromised. He tucked it back into his waterproof backpack and walked the pack over to the tree line, where it would be semi-protected. It began to rain in earnest now, lightly but steadily.

He peered down the road beyond his makeshift barrier. There was something moving in the roadside shrubbery, and he saw a flash of creamy fur. It was an animal of some sort, judging by the height of it. It was probably someone's golden retriever or yellow Labrador retriever. A head emerged from the tall grass in the ditch, and then the bear made its way slowly and leisurely onto the road.

Jonathan's first feeling wasn't fear. He felt surprise, astonishment, and disbelief. Jonathan was agog and slack-jawed. What are the chances, he pondered earnestly. Was the likelihood of a bear attack governed by the statistics he'd heard about being struck by lightning? If it happened once, was it inexplicably more likely to happen a second time? Heck, what were the chances of even seeing a spirit bear? It was the most rare of all bears. Surely that was what this one was. It was not white but yellow-gold and standing placidly in the center of the dirt road that stretched out along the river valley.

The bridge to downtown was right behind him. If he squinted, Jonathan could see it through the trees. Across the river, the backside of a concrete strip mall was visible, and the hum of cars and trucks was audible. He was close to civilization. He was close to people and to help, but was he close enough? When he had been dropped off that morning, his location had seemed urban enough. Now, though, gauging the distance, he knew instinctively that even if he sprinted as quickly as his injuries allowed him to, he wouldn't outrun that bear if it decided to charge him.

The moment dragged on. He heard the hush of the rain, the muffled city sounds, and the absence of anything else. The bear stayed where it was, looking toward him and then looking away. Jonathan, unable to feign nonchalance, worked instead at being immobile. He sat as still as he could. He thought about his lunch, which consisted of a salmon roll and two apples. It was wrapped in a plastic bag and zipped into his nylon backpack. So what, he thought. That bear can smell through concrete, I'll bet.

Then slowly and stealthily, between himself and the bear, another human being emerged from the thick roadside foliage. It was a man—a very tall man, shouldering some sort of gun. It was some sort of rifle. What the hell, Jonathan thought. The lanky man eased himself expertly out of the trees, remaining just behind a ragged roadside shrub that would partially shield him from the bear's line of sight. The man was clearly focused on the spirit bear, and his face was turned away from Jonathan. He wore the khaki pants, plaid shirt, and orange vest of a hunter. He was aiming his gun directly at the bear.

You can't shoot a goddamn spirit bear, Jonathan whispered angrily to himself. I've got to stop him!

Jonathan's voice was loud inside his head. Outwardly, he remained completely silent; he thought vaguely about the chaos that might ensue if he were to yell. This bonehead might blast off a lousy shot and injure the bear, thought Jonathan. Then he caught sight of two more people exiting the forest. They were on the side of the road that the bear had been on. He could tell that they were women. They were attired in sensible hiking clothes, but they were also wearing immediately recognizable hunting vests with shiny yellow X's on the bright orange fabric. He couldn't see them clearly because they were a little too far away. He read their body language, though. The shooter saw them and they saw the shooter. There were imperceptible nods of acknowledgement.

My God, thought Jonathan, they flushed it out for him. Sickos.

Then it dawned on him. He thought about his vision of jump-starting his career and making a splash in the environmental sustainability field. This moment was what had drawn him to Kitimat in the first place. This opportunity was the true north of his internal compass. His actions would be heroic and newsworthy. It would be the perfect launching pad. He would foil the dastardly, greedy plan of a cowardly band of poachers.

Jonathan reached down and carefully—oh so carefully—picked up the lawn chair with both of his hands. He choked up on the folded legs of the chair, creating a makeshift baseball-bat-shaped weapon. The steady patter of rain muted the noise of his footsteps. He walked heel-to-toe, creeping up behind the shooter, who was completely focused and utterly still. The two women remained transfixed by the sight of the spirit bear.

He was within a meter of the shooter with the lawn chair raised and his muscles tensed when one of the women turned around. It was Anne. Part of Jonathan's brain recognized that it was Anne. His nerve endings were committed though, and his purpose was clear.

"No, don't!" Anne shrieked.

The shooter's gun made a muted popping sound a fraction of a second before Jonathan's lawn chair connected with the side of Ian's head.

The bear loped into the forest. Ian sunk to one knee, howling.

"Sweet withering Christ! Ow!" Ian pivoted to face his attacker. "You hit me!" He assessed Jonathan reproachfully. He looked at Jonathan's bewildered young face and his long hair dripping with rain. He considered the object in his attacker's hands. "With a *lawn* chair!"

Jonathan stood in mute bewilderment. The lawn chair was still in his hand, it hung lamely half-opened at his side. He watched the two women take off running in the direction of the bear. This didn't make any sense, thought Jonathan. Anne—it was surely Anne—was talking into a two-way radio as she ran. Jonathan had a creeping suspicion that he might have intervened before fully comprehending the situation.

"Easy now," Ian said warily. "Just put down the chair and step away from it, okay? Step away from the chair. That's right."

Jonathan obediently released his grip on the lawn chair and took two halting steps backward.

"Ow, ow, ow," said Ian, sitting down heavily in the middle of the dirt road. "That really hurt! I don't think you broke my jaw but I'm going to have one hell of a bruise. Would you mind identifying yourself, you—" He struggled to find an appropriate insult. "Lawn-chair assailant?"

Jonathan looked at the rifle at Ian's side. His knowledge of firearms was limited. Looking closely, though, this rifle had a strange configuration.

"You can't shoot a spirit bear," said Jonathan. "It isn't right."

Ian regarded the young man. He was squinting and his eyes were still watering from the impact of the lawn chair. "Oh, boy," Ian said. "Oh, wow. Um, this is a dart gun, son. It shoots a hypodermic needle charged with an anaesthetic. That bear has been compromised by the oil spill, and we're relocating it to Princess Royal Island. Listen!"

The repetitive beating of a helicopter was approaching rapidly. They both looked up and scanned the sky. The helicopter appeared suddenly, the mist and fog of the rain parting for it. A long, loose red rope hung suspended from the metal bottom of the mechanical bird, which now hovered in position over a spot some two hundred meters away. A human figure was visible through an opening in the belly of the helicopter. This person manipulated something and the rope swayed back and forth. Then the red rope turned into a net, which unfurled out of view below the treetops.

The beating rhythm of the helicopter's rotors drowned out all other sound. Several minutes passed. The treetops under the helicopter bent in unnatural directions; then the helicopter swung around and flew a hundred meters away, disappearing briefly below the tree line. The helicopter soon returned, appearing to gather itself. It gained elevation, revealing a bundle of creamy fur suspended underneath it in the red net. The helicopter followed the river, heading westward toward the Douglas Channel and thence to the Pacific Ocean.

Ian and Jonathan watched and listened until the helicopter disappeared into grey mist and became inaudible. The hiss of a fine rain descended on the forest. Chipmunks were chattering somewhere close by. There was an awkward human silence.

"Wow, man. I am so incredibly sorry," said Jonathan miserably. "I just keep screwing up over and over again up here. Please don't, like, charge me with assault. I really thought you were going to kill that bear."

Ian, still seated on the ground, regarded the dejected young man standing above him. The poor kid's shoulders had collapsed, his head hung like that of a beaten dog, and he had a strangely delicate stance. He seemed fragile, as though he were made of glass.

"What's your story, kid?" asked Ian. He was aware that diminutively saying *kid* was a little insulting, but he felt justified in its usage.

Jonathan took a deep breath.

"Hold on," said Ian. "Do you know where the hospital is around here? I need to check and see if you broke my jaw."

"Kitimat Health Centre. I know the way."

"Lead on," said Ian. "You do the talking. My mouth hurts."

As they walked along in the rain, Jonathan glumly related the story of the grizzly bear attack.

"You are the luckiest—"

"I know. I know. I'm lucky I'm not dead." exclaimed Jonathan. "That's where the luck ends, though, man! I came up here to camp, meet other environmentalists, schmooze with them, and maybe talk my way into a job. I've got a shredded tent, shredded legs, and a shredded ego. Shreds, that's what I got."

Moksgm'ol

There is thirst and there is nothing to be done in the face of it but find water to drink. Many of the creeks in the Realm of Moksgm'ol are dry. The river calls to my body. These scant berries and the hapless doe I took two nights ago—they have not slaked my great hunger, and so again the river, fat with fish, beckons me. My paws are still impure but there is nothing to be done. I must descend to eat and drink. I must approach the foul domain of man once more.

I pick my route cautiously, more cautiously than is my wont. This stain upon my paws is indelible and evil. Some thing has tipped the balance between man and beast. Where once they kept to their villages and ran from the approach—nay, the mere sight—of Moksgm'ol, they now infiltrate my kingdom and do not act afraid. They have hemmed in the river that brings us plenty; they have bordered it with their grey ways of death. They venture into mountain and meadow where before they never dared. Of course I can easily elude them and keep the forest and the fern between bear and man. I can fill my belly and quench this great thirst and then retreat once more to parts untouched by man.

I reached the lowlands yesterday. I skirted a meadow of tall, brown grass. My creamy fur blended in with the thick fronds. The shrubs here are still heavy with fruit. I was able to soften the urgency of my hunger. Today is overcast. A fine rain falls, refreshing my body but intensifying my thirst. My nose leads me to some abandoned apples that are redolent of men. Desperately I eat them anyway. I come to the place where a grey way bisects the wilderness. I must cross it to reach the river. A rain-hushed quiet prevails. I proceed onto the way and survey my surroundings.

Man. A man is sitting silently and motionlessly on the road some distance from me. Is this a trap or a trick of some kind? I do not venture forward to the river, nor do I return from whence I came. I am still and stately. I am Moksgm'ol!

As I stand my ground, another man emerges from the riverside of the grey way. He is some distance from me. I stand there and stand there and then—

Pain! Ah, pain in my side, pain, I run, crash, and run from man's terrible trick. I run into the fern forest. Into the thickest undergrowth I run from pain—ah, the pain.

Ah.

This is some new trick—some trick of time. All things are slowing. All things are slowing down.

Now the edges blur on the trees. The ground blurs. Man makes sounds I have never heard, strange sounds, not frightening and harsh like most man-sounds but rhythmic and soothing.

Should I stop and sleep? Sleep with man here so close beside Moksgm'ol?

Man makes sounds I have never heard. I sleep.

Gilbert

He waits in the forest thinking about his daughter in the throes of childbirth. His new grandchild is just about to draw a first breath in the world. He prays for them and talks to Clara in his mind. Charlotte's having a little brother or sister for Jack, he tells her. She's with Walter's family. I will go to her once the bear is safe.

There is a fine, misty rain. He can hear it up in the canopy, but scarcely any moisture reaches him on the fallen log where he sits. It is a nurse log, he notes with satisfaction: an old tree whose life is over that gives her nutrients to dozens of small, spindly seedlings along her mossy green length. He runs his finger along the soft, tender needles of a young Sitka spruce.

Gilbert thinks about Anne. She is feisty in her spirit, passionate in her beliefs, and tender and affectionate in her heart. Gilbert knows that she would make a wonderful mother. Down on the floor playing dolls or cars, Clara had been a completely immersed participant in her children's imaginary worlds. She would be out in the yard or out in the forest, discovering insects hiding in the shells of ancient cedars. Anne would be such a mother, and it was not too late for Anne to have a baby—or babies. He will be fifty this year, though. His own children are having children. Could a man of his age—should a man of his age—start another family? He considered the question mathematically. If he maintained his health, he could raise another family, from the fledgling-in-the-nest stage to the stage where he watches them soar out the door on wings made strong from a loving family.

The bleeping of the two-way radio in his lap interrupts his thoughts.

It's Anne's voice. It's broken and distorted. "He's hit and he's headed toward you. Do you copy?"

"Copy that," Gilbert responds, standing and scanning the forest. He immediately spots the animal's blonde head rising and falling as it runs in his general direction at a disconcertingly rapid pace. Gilbert grows still and calm. He mentally sends out unthreatening greetings and assurances to Moksgm'ol, the great white bear of the rainforest. As if Gilbert's mental messages have been received, the bear halts, falters, turns his great head, and chews ferociously at his own flank. The bear continues charging toward the river and then stops again to bite at the foreign object embedded in his skin.

Witnessing the spirit bear's ungainly slide into unconsciousness, Gilbert is deeply disturbed. The animal crashes haphazardly through the underbrush, reeling and unsteady. Fear for his own safety recedes far behind Gilbert's sense of compassion. When Moksgm'ol the Beautiful collapses, it is a gut-wrenching sight. It is like he is dying. Gilbert is alone and closest to the smitten creature, which is contrary to the plan. The plan was to wait until they were all in sight of each other and then approach the bear and net him together.

Gary's planning wasn't foolproof, and none of the others had expected everything to go exactly according to the plan either. The bear could have strayed somewhere much more difficult to reach than this relatively open patch of second-growth forest. As it turns out, they will all be able to reach the animal on foot and not be forced to fly to another position across the river. Additionally, the spirit bear has made a bee-line for Gilbert's station in the forest, which is their optimum rendezvous point.

"Spirit bear down. Mark my location," Gilbert says into his radio. They were prepared to use GPS to find each other. It will scarcely be necessary, Gilbert thinks. The others will have a visual on him if they follow the bear's anticipated trajectory.

The sound of the increasing velocity of helicopter rotors shudders through the trees. Gilbert walks carefully to the bear's side. He kneels down beside it. The bear's paws are blackened, despoiled, and tainted by the alien substance of unrefined, dirty oil. Gilbert begins to sing a traditional song of healing. It emerges unbidden from inside him. Moksgm'ol's eyes are not closed. They are red-rimmed. The pupils roll, betraying Moksgm'ol's fear and confusion. Gilbert sings the lilting melody of his people. He has a rich and tuneful voice. The helicopter is loud, but Gilbert sings so passionately that as they close in, Anne and Jane can hear the swooping, vowel-rich syllables of his song.

Jane nods her acknowledgement and appreciation to Gilbert and then briskly sinks to one knee and begins to examine the bear. Gilbert and Anne meet each other's gaze. He continues to sing. She is serene and her face is warmed by her tiny, mysterious smile. She tells him she loves him without words.

Then Anne embraces her role as a scientist and a biologist, pressing her hand into the thick creamy fur and checking the animal's pulse. She examines the discoloration of the paws with disapproval and regret. Her smile gives way to a terse, busy little frown. Gilbert watches her confident ministrations to the powerful spirit-animal. The helicopter is now directly overhead and drowning out the healing song, but Gilbert continues to sing. A thick cable snakes out of the belly of the helicopter and descends rapidly, weighted down by the net in which the bear will be transported. Anne unclips the heavy, bulky net; she unfolds it with the confident air of a professional. They move the nearly motionless animal into the net with great difficulty.

Gary and Sandra arrive. They will not be passengers in the helicopter. Instead, they will stay behind to hook the netted bear to the cable that is hanging from the helicopter.

When they are in the air, moving toward Princess Royal Island, Gilbert tugs on Anne's sleeve. It isn't possible to have a conversation, but with facial expressions and hand gestures Gilbert manages to ask what has happened to Ian. "Long story," Anne mouths.

Moksgm'ol and the Great Bear

The Great Bear has called me to her. She must have called me, for I am walking amongst the stars. There are other creatures here with me, though I cannot see them clearly. Some unscrupulous contrivance of man has defeated me, Moksgm'ol, the White Bear of the West. I walked unhindered, feared and respected, through the rocky majesty of my homeland. In ages past I made magic in the forest at the behest of one greater than me, *and now* I have passed on to the Sky World.

She appears to me. She is One-bear. She is Every-bear. Some unrecognized feeling wells up inside me. I bow my head. I bend my forelegs. I prostrate myself before her. Then I know the feeling is humility. I am humbled by she who created us all.

After a time, I dare to raise my eyes and behold her once more. I feel fear and dismay. There is a man with her. He is a male and he is naked. He stands beside her. He is small and insignificant in her presence, yet he is familiar enough with her to touch her and immerse his hand in a tuft of her iridescent fur. My body fills with a swift current of attack impulses. My teeth long to bite. My claws long to shred and remove the threat of this man—this representative of my untimely fate.

An ancient voice resonates inside my skull and the drive to attack the man disappears. There is another sound, the sound I had never heard which lulled me to sleep. Somehow

I recognize the sound now, it is the sound of singing. The man begins to sing a haunting chant. It is strangely calming. It is a deep, not-unpleasant music. The Great Bear sways to the rhythm of the man's chant. In spite of myself, I find that I am moving to his song as well.

The stars around the Great Bear and the man become brighter and brighter until I can no longer make out their shapes. Everything becomes a white glare. The chanting continues. I am in a deep sleep. Perhaps I shall wake or perhaps this sleep is eternal. In any event, whatever the outcome, I am no longer distraught. I am at peace.

Dispersal

There was a soft white flannel bundle of big brown curious eyes and a dramatic shock of jet-black hair. Two perfect, miniature hands were randomly clenching and flexing, popping out of the cradle of her grandfather's arms. Seven adults and a newborn surrounded Gilbert's kitchen table, a comfortable crowd in his little cabin.

"What time was she born?" Sandra asked.

"Eleven in the morning," Charlotte answered through an expansive yawn. "Gary was flying Dad up to Terrace right then. I was so amazed when he walked in that he had already guessed her name!"

"Aurora," said Anne. "She is so beautiful."

A session of general cooing and admiration ensued. Charlotte's husband, Walter, had only recently dropped his father-in-law, wife, and newborn daughter off at the cabin. He and Jack, who was almost two years old, had gone to buy groceries while Grandpa showed off his new granddaughter. Walter and Charlotte were moving back to Kitimat. The immediate crisis of the spill had passed.

"So, how is our bear?" Gilbert asked eventually.

"Everything indicates that the bear is excellent," Gary answered. "The transceiver shows lots of normal, vigorous movement and activity."

Anne opened her mouth to address Jane, who had already anticipated the question. "Tlingit is also doing well," said Jane, smiling. "Ian and I are flying back to Churchill in two days to resume our research there. When can we expect you, Anne?"

"Uh," Anne bit her lower lip, "my plans are a little up in the air right now. There's a lot of, uh, compiling and writing that I can do from here without compromising my position in Churchill." She glanced at Gilbert. He was engrossed with the warm little human in his arms. "How's your face, Ian?" Anne asked, diverting the conversation.

"Not bad," Ian answered, lifting his hand to gingerly caress his right cheek. A purplish yellow bruise extended from cheekbone to jawline.

"Looks terrible," said Sandra. "Hey kid," she addressed Jonathan. "Are you hanging around for awhile? Gary and I need a decent batter for our slow-pitch team."

"Just don't bring your pet grizzly," added Gary.

Jonathan laughed. "Yes, I'm staying in Kitimat for awhile. I got a job!" he crowed. "In my field!"

"You don't say," said Gilbert, interrupting his study of Aurora. "Doing what? And for whom?"

Jonathan closed his mouth, embarrassed. He could scarcely believe this turn of events himself. He had always imagined working for Greenpeace or the World Wildlife Foundation. He had always imagined working for the environment with an organization that shared his values and beliefs. He had learned a lot from Ian in a short span of time, and Ian had felt a sudden intimacy with the young man, due only in part to the righteous indignation and moral superiority of the attacked toward the attacker. In Jonathan, Ian saw himself a decade earlier: young, naive, impractical, impatient, and poised to save the world. Ian took it upon himself to give the young man a series of tutorials on resume distribution, open-mindedness, and effecting change from the inside.

Ian had also interrogated Jonathan on his impressions of Anne and Gilbert's closeness. Learning that the couple were evidently in love, Ian had gently suggested that Jonathan find somewhere else to unfurl his bedroll, convalesce, and get his feet on the ground.

Gilbert was smiling and waiting for an answer from Jonathan, who was blushing. "Jonathan is going to work for Elba Energy," Ian interrupted before Jonathan could respond. "He's going to do some impact studies and a little liaising with the media. He's going to live at Little Ted's until he gets his first paycheque."

An uncomfortable silence greeted this announcement. Sandra finally broke it.

"Wow. You're leaving the Force to go to work for the Dark Side," she said.

"That's not fair," said Ian. "Now, more than ever, companies like Elba Energy need employees with educations like Jonathan's. If they had been employing some decent environmental sustainability assessors prior to building the pipeline, they probably wouldn't be getting slapped with a multimillion-dollar cleanup bill right now—not to mention the lawsuits that are inevitably being filed in court as we speak."

"But Elba Energy is just going to find the cheapest way to put a Band-Aid on this thing and keep selling crude oil overseas. To work for them is to make other environmental disasters like this one way more likely to happen," said Sandra.

"Perhaps this accident will precipitate change," said Jane.

"Yeah, right," Anne scoffed. "Tomorrow we'll all start riding horses and bicycles and Elba Energy will switch to manufacturing solar panels."

"Change is hard for humanity," said Gilbert. "You know what it's like? It's like..." He glanced down at Aurora, who had fallen asleep and was now snoring gently in his arms. "It's like birth. Think about it: Charlotte's body is the planet. Charlotte's body is the world."

"I resent that, Dad," Charlotte interjected. "I gained a little extra weight during this pregnancy but it was nothing—*nothing* —compared to how much I gained with Jack."

"You're beautiful," Gilbert told his daughter over the laughter. "You're the world. Inside you is humanity today, and it's growing. It's gestating. We gain knowledge. We gain experience. Ultimately, we realize, though, that all of that knowledge and experience isn't going to do us any good unless we push on out of this comfortable body we're in and go out into completely different and scary unknown places outside. The process of simply getting out there is going to hurt."

"Our awareness of the environment, our gratitude for the natural world, our desire to live more synchronously with the forces and rhythms of nature—all of these things have been improving and maturing. Fifty years ago North Americans were proud of their disposable goods. Today, they're proud if they recycle. It's not enough, though. We need really big and really strong—"

"Contractions," Charlotte supplied, sighing and groaning the way that only someone who had just experienced contractions could sigh and groan.

"Precisely," said Gilbert. "I think we can all extrapolate from there." Before anyone could get started talking about forceps and episiotomies, he said, "When we're out there in that new place, breathing that unfamiliar air, we'll develop alternate energies, use light rapid transit, and grow organic food in our own backyards. We'll create economies around these things that work and make sense. And we'll look back on that time inside the womb and wonder that we were ever there."

* * *

The first snow fell on a night in late October. A few tentative snowflakes descended in the darkness of the early hours of the morning; more snowflakes joined them until the white, powdery precipitation was falling steadily. By dawn, Kitimat was covered in a bright white sheet. The snow announced itself to Gilbert first through his sense of hearing. Sounds came to his ears in the muffled, muted way that the sounds of a town travel through curtains of snow. His ears also knew it had snowed by the shocking silence of the birds. Even his namesake, Crow, who usually had a lot of loud, sarcastic opinions about everything, was perched in a tree somewhere, amazed. His beady eyes were bulging and his beak was firmly shut.

Gilbert lay very still, immobilized by the lush, warm body of his lover. A generous breast was snugged up to his shoulder, and a smooth, fragrant arm was draped across his chest. She slept soundly, her nose whistling a little as she inhaled. The bedroom window was open a centimeter or two to provide fresh air through the night. The air was crisp. It was as though the snow on its descent had scrubbed the atmosphere.

The snowy hush was broken by the sound of a vehicle approaching and stopping nearby. He heard the metallic creak-and-slam of a car door opening and closing. Gilbert listened. Several minutes passed. Then he heard a light, reluctant tapping on his cabin door. He gingerly lifted Anne's arm and slid from beneath her, disturbing her sleep a little in spite of his efforts.

"I love you," she murmured, as he tucked blankets around her solicitously.

"I know," he whispered back. He slid into the previous day's jeans and plaid shirt, which had been expressly draped over a chair for stoking the morning fire.

It was Max at the door. He was leaning patiently on the threshold. Gilbert let him in, wordlessly but with a welcoming smile. Gilbert busied himself making coffee as his son removed his snow-encrusted boots and then padded to the kitchen table in socks. He sat there expectantly, anticipating the hot beverage. Time slid sideways and Max momentarily became an awkward teenager, a restless young boy, and an irresistibly round and red-cheeked baby. When the coffee was ready, Gilbert poured it and came to sit with Max, who was once again a young adult with a serious face.

"Aurora looks like Mom," Max began. Gilbert nodded in agreement. His infant granddaughter, only a couple of weeks into her journey on earth, didn't resemble anyone but herself yet, Gilbert thought, but he was glad that Max saw Clara in his sister's baby.

"You have a girlfriend," Max continued. It was a statement of fact rather than an accusation.

Gilbert nodded again. "Anne," he supplied, looking briefly at the bedroom door to acknowledge her presence.

"This spill is a damn shame," Max said eventually. "Guess I was wrong about it never happening."

"Business has picked up at the tire shop, though?" Gilbert asked.

"Yeah, sure," Max answered. "Elba Energy trucks are getting their winters on today. It's going to be a really busy one."

Gilbert nodded and sipped his coffee.

"The fact is, though, Dad," Max continued, "I don't want to work there for the rest of my life. I never told you this, but the fact is I was hoping to gradually get into working as a fishing guide around here."

"You'd be great, Max," Gilbert said earnestly. He had fished in oceans and rivers with his son since Max could walk, and in his biased opinion Max was a particularly gifted fisherman. He was quiet, observant, and patient. He was friendly enough to work with the public and stern enough to tell greedy tourists that they were over their catch limit.

"Yeah, well, it's going to be a while before anyone wants to come fish around here," said Max bitterly. "I really didn't think it was going to happen. I thought that they had it figured out so that it wouldn't happen. I guess I understand why you were so against it. The whole time, I thought you were just doing it for Mom."

"I was protesting for all of us—your mother, you, Charlotte, and her family—and I was doing it for me too. And I was doing it for the bears," said Gilbert.

"Just the bears?" Max asked.

"And Salmon and Raven and Crow and Wolf and Frog and Beaver," Gilbert answered. "You know, everyone."

"Yeah. Well it's good to see you, Dad." Max tipped his mug and gulped down the remainder of his coffee. "I've got to get to work." He stood up, walked to the door, and busied himself pushing his feet and thick woollen socks into his snow boots.

Gilbert followed his son to the door. They hugged.

"I'll stop by again soon, Dad, to meet Anne," said Max.

"That'd be nice." Gilbert watched Max get into his truck and drive away. He watched until the taillights disappeared around a corner. Then everything was snow-covered and quiet once more.

Tlingit

The nightmare of the man-things is over. There is ice everywhere. Everywhere, there is ice. The ice is the same as memories and the same as earlier times. The World of the Bear is everywhere. My stomach is shrieking and crying out, but already I see Seal slither from the ice through a hole into the water. Toward this hole I move, and yes, yes, I push with my paws and the ice is heavy, thick, and holding.

The patience of the Great Bear is with me. I am so grateful for the gift of patience that she has given me. I stand where Seal soon will come. It is cold! O perfect coldness around me. A light snow is dusting my fur. I lick and it is so good—perfect, yes perfect. The time to wait for the water to turn hard is over. The waiting is over. Ice is here. The miracle of ice is all around.

Quickly it happens when it does. Seal pops out of the water from the hole onto the ice. Seal never sees the white bear of winter. With merciful speed I bite where Seal's head meets Seal's body. Thank you, Seal, for your life. Thank you, Seal, for the gift of your life to strengthen my life. Oh, thank you. There is a sudden spray of red blood on white snow.

I devour this animal—slash, rip, gulp—and find a new opening for Seal, where I wait to take one more animal and eat it as well. Two seals. My belly is full for the first time since before K'ytuk was inside me. The panic of having no food and no ice recedes. The panic recedes and the calmness comes.

A bitter north wind blows, freezing what it touches. O north wind, your sting and bite sustain me. The sharp needles of the snowstorm blow in white curtains everywhere. O K'ytuk, here, in this frozen place of white bears, you could have lived. My K'ytuk, I will always remember you.

Moksgm'ol

I wake to the rhythm of surf crashing onto rocks and the distant screaming of gulls. I have been sleeping a long time, and I can feel this in the heaviness of my body. Unfamiliar with my surroundings, I stand and raise my head, opening my senses to learn everything I can.

The air is pure and unadulterated. I smell the clean smells of forest, ocean, and fern. I can detect late fall berries, a hint of fresh fish, and moist earth sweetly composting layers of leaves and teeming with worms. My nostrils quiver in delight. I listen, rotating my ears and turning my head. I can hear Squirrel scrabbling on bark and scampering from branch to branch. Ah, I can hear the heavier hoof-beats of Deer! My tongue moistens with saliva. Moksgm'ol, Great Hunter, shall feast before the day is done!

What is this place? My senses tell me a delightful story—a story of absences. The strange stench of recent days is almost gone. The smallest remnant of that terrible smell remains. I realize with dismay that it emanates from the tainted, black-tinted longer hairs of my own paws. Still, with each morning it recedes. Today it is very faint, almost completely obscured by the many strong, natural perfumes of the earth.

I do not recognize this stream or these rocks. I do not recognize this shore or these trees. I have woken into an unfamiliar paradise, or perhaps I am dreaming and I will wake once more *to men and their machines. I think not. I feel as if I have woken now from an impossible dream—a dream in which I soared above the trees and rivers like Eagle. In the dream there was a song, a haunting chant. I was touched by the very hands of men and then accompanied in a flight through the sky by an infernal flying man-machine.*

Impossible! I stretch my limbs and yawn. A loud and satisfied sound comes from deep within me as I do so. Small creatures— mice, birds, and snakes—flee at the bold bear-sound I have made. Yes. I am Moksgmʼol, the Spirit Bear, returned to my kingdom after exile. My mettle tested, my obstacles overcome, and my difficulties surmounted, I emerge. I am Moksgmʼol the Fierce! I am Moksgmʼol, the Brave!

I run with wild abandon through this new domain that the Great Bear has provided for me!

The Great Bear Welcomes Yukuai

The bright daylight of the sky above my enclosure fades gradually and I am immersed in total darkness. The blackness is absolute. The great weight of my earthly form—four heavy black limbs and my white barrel of a body—descends from me. My mass sinks beneath the shell of my body and drifts away. The chatter of human voices, which has plagued me for all of these many days, is at long last silenced. I am suspended in a dream of lightless and weightless peace.

The dream goes on and on. I am aware. My soul is intact and the Zen of nothingness, the absence of all stimuli, is intensely pleasurable. If this is all there is—if this sensation extends into limitless time—then I should be a grateful bear.

At an indeterminate moment, though, there is a change. Light comes little by little, illuminating everything ever so gradually. It is sunlight, and it dapples a clearing of tall, swaying, blue-green cylinders. I am in a forest of towering wet green stalks. There are rich earth-smells, and the air is full of crisp chlorophyll. They must be hollow, these softly swaying stalks. Low, beautiful musical tones sound out whenever two of them touch. I am in some earthly place, yet the comfort of weightlessness remains. I am aware of the parameters of what used to be my body.

A Bear, larger than me, appears beside me. I am not startled or distressed, but I cannot clearly make out where this other bear begins and where she ends. She thinks and her thoughts are known to me—not the soft black tufts that used to be my ears, but my core. Her thoughts are known to the nucleus of the cell of me.

The bamboo groves of your youth, Yukuai—you didn't dream them, after all. I thought you would want to see them once more before we go onward.

The heart of me is a place of feeling. It swells with an entire galaxy of planets of emotions. I can feel its perfect natural

beauty and its sweet familiarity. The unquestionable rightness of my conscious self in this place surges through the
part of me that is aware. The grove becomes more tangible:
running water over smooth stones and sparkling dew drop-
lets on sweet blue-green leaves. The utter rightness of the
spirit of Yukuai being reunited with this place is accompanied, though, by a great and terrible sadness—a sombre
understanding of the sorrow of the knowledge of what might
have been.

Yukuai, the Bear gives me to understand, *long you have
suffered, and your earthly journey has been a vexatious, ardu-
ous one.*

In a flash, I compress pain, fire, flames, screams, cold,
hunger, confinement, illness, mockery, fear, loneliness, and
boredom. I make all this into a ball of anguish and I push this
ball toward the form of the bear beside me.

Yes, the Great Bear acknowledges, *this reality is your truth,
Yukuai. There is no might-have-been. There is only what is and
what was.*

Tear-stars sparkle in the Great Bear's eyes.

Linger here in this place and be healed.

Time ceases to be quantifiable. Among this tuneful movement of tall bamboo, I simply am. I exist here in perfect comfort, stripped of all biology, never hungry or cold or stricken
by any physical sensations. Small black butterflies make their
erratic way amongst the plants. Little white bellflowers in the
undergrowth emit a soothing perfume. An ever-present sun

warms the imaginary fur of my back. A never-ending breeze cools and soothes a body that doesn't exist. Without irony or falsehood, I become that for which I was named. I am Happy.

Either a million years or mere moments pass. It doesn't matter. The knowledge of this perfect bamboo grove is a balm that heals all the sores of concrete cages and the welts of the firestorm. It eases, though it doesn't erase, the years of my earthly existence.

The Great Bear comes again. Her form is beside mine and I am given to experiencing a peace that living beings cannot know.

Come, Yukuai. Come walk with me among the stars.

Made in the USA
Charleston, SC
19 January 2013